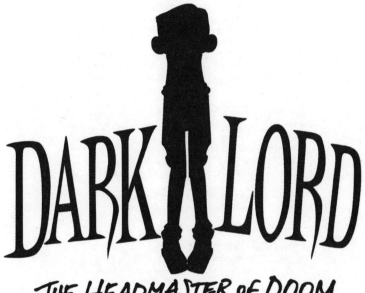

DARK LORD

THE HEADMASTER of DOOM

ORCHARD BOOKS

First published in Great Britain in 2017 by The Watts Publishing Group

1 3 5 7 9 10 8 6 4 2

A CIP catalogue record for this book
is available from the British Library.

ISBN 978 1 40834 142 1
Printed and bound by CPI Group (UK) Ltd, Croydon, CR0 4YY
The paper and board used in this book are
made from wood from responsible sources.

Orchard Books
An imprint of Hachette Children's Group
Part of The Watts Publishing Group Limited
Carmelite House
50 Victoria Embankment
London EC4Y 0DZ

An Hachette UK Company
www.hachette.co.uk
www.hachettechildrens.co.uk

DARK LORD

THE HEADMASTER OF DOOM

JAMIE THOMSON

ORCHARD

CONTENTS

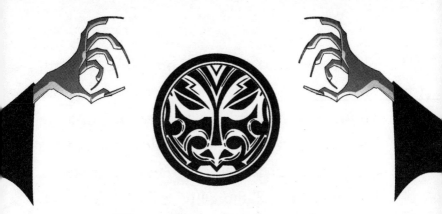

The Dark Lord
Speaks

It's possible that – incredible to imagine – some worthless humans may not have read my previous works of astonishing magnificence, to wit, *Dark Lord: The Teenage Years*, *Dark Lord: A Fiend in Need* and *Dark Lord: Eternal Detention* (yes, that's right – Eternal Detention). If you are one of those worthless humans, here is a summary of previous events:

Once I was a mighty Dark Lord, but I was defeated in battle and exiled to your wretched planet by that tiresome meddling Wizard, Hasdruban the White. Even worse than that (I know, how could it be?) he cursed me into the body of a puny human boy child! I tried to tell everyone I was the Dark Lord but, being stupid humans, you all thought I said 'Dirk Lloyd' instead, and that became my name. Being sickening do-gooders (mostly), you humans forced me to go to school, and live with foster parents. Sigh.

At least I made some friends – or lackeys, as I prefer to call them – Sooz and Christopher.

At first, I considered conquering your wretched planet, but that didn't work out, so I turned my evil genius to the task of getting home to the Darklands, where I belonged. I cast a great spell to send me back, but it went wrong (not my fault, of course!) and instead of propelling me back to the Darklands, it sent my friend Sooz…

Dark Lord: A Fiend in Need tells the story of

how Sooz arrived in the Darklands. Amazingly, she was able to take over the Iron Tower and become the Moon Queen of the Darklands, where she claims that she ruled in peace and harmony, making new friends and allies. Bah, more do-gooding nonsense! Hasdruban didn't care either – he tricked Sooz and imprisoned her in his White Tower. Not content with that, he also sent the White Witch, disguised as a nanny, to finish me off on earth. But me and my ~~friend~~ lackey Chris turned the tables on her, and found a way to get to the Darklands.

It was tough but we bluffed our way into the White Tower and freed Sooz, but I had to cast a very dangerous spell to get her out, and it looked like I was going to die! Sooz and Chris had to give me the Essence of Evil, the black goo I'd coughed up when I first fell to earth. It turned me back into a twelve-feet-tall, hoofed and horned Dark Lord, which was great! It was good to be home, as it were. But then I just got more and more… well, evil, until finally I lost it completely and locked Chris and Sooz in the Dungeons of Doom. (Not my best moment, I admit.) Anyway, Chris and Sooz used a special magic crystal to propel us all (including the monster Gargon and the Paladin Rufino) back to earth. Along the way, I turned back into the boy Dirk, coughing up the Evil Essence once more, which was a relief, really, I can tell you – it's such an effort to be evil. Anyway, we were home, and all seemed well – except that the White Wizard had got there before us, taken over the school and made himself the new headmaster, Dr Hasdruban…

He then proceeded to make my life miserable with constant detentions, kidnapping plans, assassination attempts and so on. He even brought the Black Hag – a hideous, poison-nailed witch from the Darklands – over to murder me!

But then the White Witch realised I wasn't

really the bad guy any more – Hasdruban was. She helped us get back to the Darklands to steal the Black Hag's Tears – said to give any who drank a Tear a terrible kind of empathy (it's complicated). Along the way, Sooz got turned into a mighty Vampire Queen! I preferred her like that but my friend lackey Chris said we had to 'rescue' her. Bah, whatever. Anyway, we saved her, stole one of the Hag's Tears and returned to earth. I tricked Hasdruban into taking the Tear and he suddenly became all nice and sympathetic! He's a kindly old fellow now, and one of the best headmasters we'd ever had. Who'd'a thought it?

Now everything's 'hunky dory', as you witless humans say.

Or is it?

Detention, Darklands Style

'AAAAaaaarghhhh!' screamed Agrash as he plummeted into the vast, black pit. His old friend, Skabber Stormfart, had ignored his pitiful cries for mercy and with a whispered 'Sorry, mate' had thrown him in anyway,

Agrash smashed into the bottom of the pit and lay there for a moment, breathing in the pain. Thankfully, something had broken his fall. It hurt, but no bones seemed broken and he was still alive. He felt around. He'd landed on a pile of old straw and dirty clothes, a heap of discarded Orc and Goblin army uniforms, by the looks of them – or rather the smell of them. He got to his feet. It was dark, but not completely. There was light from a nearby lamp resting on some kind of table. Agrash made his way through the piles of old clothes that littered the floor. The table was actually a desk and a chair. Yes, a desk. Just like a schoolboy's desk back on earth. Agrash sat upon it. On the desk in front of him was a sheaf of papers and a pencil – a pencil from earth.

On top of the sheaf was a note, written in thin, scratchy-looking letters, as if a spider had dipped its feet in ink and scuttled across the page. It read:

AGRASH SNOTRIPPER

Your punishment for your gross insubordination and sending a message out of class will be:

1. Imprisonment in the black pit of a thousand lines

2. Writing out one thousand times: 'I will not disobey the true Dark Lord or send messages in class'

A drip of snot fell off the edge of Agrash's improbably long nose and splashed on to the paper, leaving a green-tinged stain.

'Oops!' said Agrash, trying to rub it off with his sleeve.

Agrash reviewed his sentence. Imprisonment and a thousand lines. At least it wasn't a death sentence, as he'd been expecting. The trouble was that it was ambiguous. Did it mean imprisonment until he'd written out his one thousand lines, after which he'd be released? Or imprisonment and one thousand lines, in which case who knew when he'd be released?

There was only one way to find out.

Agrash was about to begin writing out his lines when he heard a snorting whimper from nearby. He looked over. Sitting on a tiny stool in front of a little desk was the hulking form of a seven-foot, scaled and fanged demon with wings, tiny red eyes and big taloned hands, trying to hold on to his little pencil. His wings had been padlocked together, so he could not fly.

It was Gargon – Dread Gargon, the Hewer of Limbs and Captain of the Legions of Dread, the Dark Lord's most loyal servant. The original Dark Lord, Dirk's most loyal servant, that was. And here he was, crying in the dark. Agrash made his way over.

'What's wrong, Gargy?' said Agrash in his squeaky Goblin voice.

Gargon turned to look at Agrash, his red eyes even redder with tears. 'Agrash, old friend, is good to see you,' rasped Gargon in a voice like shattered pebbles.

'What happened?' said Agrash.

'That new Dark Lord, he try tell me what to do, but I refuse, I stay loyal to Dirk!'

'Yeah, yeah, brains were never your strong point, were they, Gargy?' said Agrash.

'Maybe – but you here too,' said Gargon.

'Ah, yes… Good point!' said Agrash.

'Dark Headmaster throw me into pit and give me one thousand lines. Say he not release Gargon until I finish punishment!' said Gargon.

'Well, that's not so bad!'

''Cep' Gargon…'

'Except Gargon what?' said Agrash.

'Gargon not able to read. Or write… So Gargon trapped here forever!'

'Ah, of course! Hmm… I see. Well, don't worry, Gargy, I can write them out for you.'

'Really?' said Gargon, brightening up a little. Well, inasmuch as a seven-foot tall, winged demon thing could brighten up.

'Sure – you see, I think we're going to be stuck down here together for quite a while,' said Agrash.

After all, they were in detention, Darklands style…

Evil Comes Home to Roost

The Dark Lord paced slowly down the Great Hall of Gloom towards the Throne of Skulls. He was at least twelve feet tall, but bony and narrow. As he walked, his long, thin legs cracked and clicked every time he bent a knee. His long, ragged black cloak hung down his back like tattered wings and on his head was a flat, black hat, like an old-fashioned headmaster's mortarboard. In one hand he held a long, curved cane that he swished and swooshed around as if ever eager to beat someone with it. The cane was black and shiny, like polished ebony.

As he walked on, lamps burst into flame on the pillars lining the way. The light revealed ranks of Goblin soldiers lining the route, dressed…well, dressed in shorts and little caps, each marked with the symbol of their Household Legion. They wore what looked like school blazers but they were made of hardened leather. At their belts were outsized schoolboy catapults, used to hurl pebbles and stones that could be as deadly as a rock from a sling at close range. They also carried short stabbing swords that looked like nothing more than schoolboys' steel rulers, but with edges sharpened to deadly effect. They stared straight ahead, fearful of this new Dark Lord's wrath and the strokes of his terrible black cane, hoping he would not notice them as he passed.

His gait was strange and ungainly, his head bobbing up and down in time with the popping and cracking of his knees. Ahead, the throne loomed out of the gloom – the Throne of Skulls.

As the Dark Lord neared, the skulls began to wail and screech, like lost souls forever trapped in a lightless Hades. The Dark Lord ascended the dais that led up to the throne and sat upon it, and the skulls moaned a low moan of sonorous despair. As he sat, a figure emerged from behind the throne to stand just below him, taking her place on his left hand side. She was dressed in long, ragged black lace, with a strange, cobwebbed black headdress, a ripped-up black veil, and arm-length tattered black velvet gloves. Her fingers ended in long, iron talons dripping with venom. It was the Lady Grieve, also known as the Black Hag, and the deadliest witch to ever walk the Darklands.

'Greeting, Deputy Headmistress,' said the Dark Lord, in a cracked voice – a voice that sounded as if it were ever balancing on the edge of total madness.

'Greetings, Dark Headmaster,' said the Black Hag with a nod of her veiled head, her voice like dry sand running through an hourglass.

The Dark Lord looked up – his eyes were as black as the blackest night, his face long and thin and gaunt, with an elongated, bony chin that protruded down over his neck. His face was sickly pale, but the chin was red and raw.

'Where is my Head Boy?' said the Dark Lord.

'I'm right 'ere, Headmaster,' said a large Orc as he stepped up to the throne. He was dressed as the others, in cap, armoured blazer and shorts, save that he also wore a cape.

'Report card, please, Skabber,' said the Dark Lord. (For the Head Boy was indeed Skabber Stormfart, Champion Orc of the Darklands.)

'Yes, sir, here you go!' He handed a sheet of paper to the Dark Lord…

And gulped.

The Dark Lord began to read.

'Agrash has been sent to the Pit of a Thousand

Lines for punishment – good, good,' said the Dark Lord. 'He's still loyal to that dreadful boy, Dirk Lloyd, isn't he? Well, he'll learn the price of talking back to the teachers. Wait a minute… No, no, you don't spell it like that, boy! And this grammar here, it's awful…'

Skabber blinked up at the Dark Lord. 'I'm sorry, Dark Headmaster, but Agrash… he was the only one that could write proper, sir!'

'You ignorant boy! If you weren't the best bully I've ever had, I'd cane you myself! Now get out of my sight and fetch me the Lamia, Lucina!'

'Yes, sir, right away, sir!' said Skabber.

He hurried away as fast as he could, peering back over his shoulder to check the Dark Lord's cane was still by his side.

The Dark Lord put a hand up to his chin and stroked it, a movement eerily similar to the way his nemesis, Dirk Lloyd, did it – except that as soon as he'd begun, the Dark Headmaster winced in pain, for his chin was red and raw and sore.

He put his hands down on the armrests of his throne. The skulls wailed, heralding a speech, and the Dark Lord called out in a loud voice, addressing all the assembled Orcs and Goblins.

'Listen Goblin girls and boys! I have reorganised the school…err…the army. Instead of regiments, you will arrange your troops according to these houses: Telling Off to Death House, the House of Doom, 666 of the Best House, Sharpened Pencils of Megadeath House, and Black Hag House.'

'Yes, Headmaster of Doom!' chorused the assembly.

'Each house will have a House Master, to be determined by me, and also Black Prefects, to be chosen by the House Master or Mistress.'

Something began to slither its way towards the Throne of Skulls. A large serpent came into view, its snake body undulating as it drew closer. But instead of a snake's head, it had the head and torso of a woman – a beautiful woman with long dark brown hair and grey-green eyes.

'You summoned me, Dark Headmaster,' said the snake woman in a rich voice. She was a Lamia, a special monster that was half human, half gigantic snake. And if that wasn't horrible enough, she also had the power to mimic the form of others, to appear as she wished to the beholder.

'Ah, welcome, Lucina the Lamia. I have a task for you!' said the Dark Lord.

'Yes, sir?' said the Lamia.

'Can you take on the form of the White Witch, Hasdruban's deputy?'

'Oh yes, my Dark Headmaster, yes indeed,' said Lucina, and she began to change shape. Soon she wore the form of the White Witch – long white hair, pale alabaster skin, eyes so grey they were almost white…and no eyebrows. She could mimic clothes too – long white robes, trimmed with white lace and a white veil.

'Ah yes, a perfect likeness. Hasdruban won't be able to tell the difference, will he?

'No, my Dark Lord and Headmaster,' said Lucina. Unfortunately, Lucina couldn't mimic voices – but that didn't matter because the White Witch was mute: she never spoke. The witch communicated instead with little notes.

'Excellent. Now go and kidnap the old fool. Lure him into a trap and then bring him back here. I think it's time he was given lodgings in the Dungeons of Doom!'

Bad News
Travels Fast

Dave the Storm Crow squawked in pain as he crash-landed on to Dirk's desk in a flurry of dust and feathers. Dirk recoiled in shock. Behind him, in the middle of the room, a dark opening in the very fabric of space itself closed up with a gloopy pop.

The Crow bumbled to its feet, shaking its head groggily and flapping its wings in indignation. Out fell a little pebble. Dirk frowned. It looked like Dave had been hit by a small stone, such as might have been fired from a schoolboy's catapult. But that must have happened in the Darklands, just before the Crow entered the portal between the worlds on its way here to earth. Who would dare to shoot at the Dark Lord's messenger, his Harbinger of Doom?

Dirk held the tiny stone up to the light. It had been engraved with words in the Black Tongue, the language of the Darklands used by Goblins and Orcs and a host of other even more unsavoury creatures.

'Eat it!' read the message.

Typical Orcish humour, thought Dirk, with an appreciative grin. Then his grin faded. Why would one of his minions try to shoot Dave?

Not that they'd been very successful – the crow was a little groggy but other than that, he seemed fine. He squawked once more, blinking up at Dirk, his black eyes glowing and his feathers shining like coal. Dirk smiled down at him. Crows were so beautiful to look at, and he

loved the sound of their desolate cry. This Crow
was special. He was a Storm Crow and he could
fly anywhere, even across dimensions, as long
as he was bearing a message for the Dark Lord.
After smoothing down Dave's ruffled feathers
and feeding him a worm or two from the jar on
his desk (yes, Dirk kept a jar of worms labelled
'Wormy Wyrms'), Dirk hurriedly unfurled the
parchment message attached to the Crow's leg.
It was from his Goblin lieutenant, Agrash, who
he'd left in charge of the Iron Tower of Despair
back home in the Darklands. It had been weeks
since Dirk had heard anything from home…

Master, it is I Agrash!
Terrible news – he has seized control!
There is a new Dark Lord in the Iron
Tower and…wait…something comes…
it's… NOOOOO!
Fly Dave, fly!

Dirk frowned. He? Who is 'he' and how dare he seize my Iron Tower! he thought. He spoke out loud. 'Doesn't this fool know who I am? Whoever "he" is, he will suffer the full torment of my wrath!'

Dirk surged to his feet and steepled his fingers together. 'There can be only one Dark Lord and that Dark Lord is me!' he said loudly. Then he put back his head and laughed his Evil Laugh.

'MWAH, HAH, HAH!' echoed around the room, out into the corridor beyond and throughout the rest of the house.

'Oh do be quiet, Dirk!' cried a voice from downstairs. 'I'm trying to listen to *The Archers*!'

Dirk raised his eyes and sighed. But then he scowled. He put a hand up to his chin. This was no laughing matter, it was serious. It sounded like his throne had been usurped. He had to act.

'There's nothing for it. I absolutely have to return home to the Darklands, and as soon as possible,' he muttered. 'I think this upstart usurper needs to taste the ravening flames of my Great Ring of Power!'

Dirk held up his hand and looked at the ring he wore. Here on earth it was powerless, but back home in the Darklands, it radiated magic power. Its runes glowed with energy, and he could fire bolts of destructive energy from it, time and time again. It made him mighty, indeed!

But how to get back there? There were no Anathema Crystals (special magical crystals that, when smashed, propelled everyone within a few feet to another dimension, like the Darklands or back to earth) in his possession. Nor did he have one of those Magic Holes (literally a magic hole that you could lay out on the ground, step into and travel to whatever location you shouted as you fell – as long as you'd visited that place at least once before).

The White Wizard Dr Hasdruban – now headmaster of Whiteshields School – had some Magic Holes, though, and he was always happy to lend some to Dirk. Once, he'd been a fanatical Wizard dedicated to destroying Dirk[1] at all costs, but now he was a kindly old man, who divided his time between earth and the Darklands. Here he was a dedicated headmaster, and back in their home world the wise ruler of the Commonwealth of Good Folk.

It was time to visit the old fool. As it was school half term he'd probably be at home. Shouldn't be a problem. After all, for the first time ever there was true peace in the Darklands. Orcs and Goblins traded with humans and elves – they even talked and hung out together.

Well, every now and again.

Anyway, the last thing they needed was a new Evil One in the Tower of Despair. There'd be blood and death and war and all that business all over again! Dirk was confident that Hasdruban would help him fix that.

---

[1] *As told in book 3,* Dark Lord: Eternal Detention

Dirk stepped out into the corridor of the Purejoies' home (his foster parents were Mr and Mrs Purejoie) and into Chris's room, where Chris and Sooz were hanging out, listening to Sooz's Goth music band, Soozie and the Nightwalkers.

'What do you think, Dirk?' said Sooz. 'It's my latest song – "Love Under the Dark Moon of Sorrows!"'

'Not bad, my little vampire,' said Dirk, 'but we have more important things to worry about.'

'Don't tell me, you've got quadruple detention – again!' said Christopher with a laugh.

'Hah! I wish! There's no time to explain. You two, come with me!' said Dirk in commanding tones as he turned on his heel and began to march out of the room.

'How rude!' hissed Sooz.

'Typical,' muttered Chris, but they both got up and followed him out.

Dirk strode purposefully for the front door.

'Where are we going?' said Christopher.

'To see Hasdruban – we've got to get to the Darklands as soon as we can!'

'What?' said Sooz. 'I've got a concert tomorrow…'

'And I'm in the school play!'

'Pah, you will have to put aside your petty human concerns in all their tawdry mundanity, for we have things to do! You, Christopher, shall be my lieutenant again, and you, Sooz, must take up the mantle of the Moon Queen once more, for we travel to jeopardy and adventure most perilous!'

'What – number four, Beeches Close?' said Chris.

'Eh?' replied Dirk.

'The Headmaster's house. 4 Beeches Close,' said Sooz, laughing. 'That's where we're travelling to, right?'

A Plan Full of Holes

4 Beeches Close was a little rickety seventeenth-century cottage at the end of a cul de sac, its garden looking out over a small wood with a stream running through it. It was pretty much just as you would imagine a kindly old wizard's house to be; an idyllic retreat with deer that came up to the back fence for food, and a lovingly tended herb garden. It was a house that gave off an aura of peace and love.

Dirk hated it.

Dirk, with Sooz and Chris in his wake, strode up to the old oak door and rapped hard upon it. But the door was already slightly ajar, and now it swung inward with a creak.

'That's odd,' said Chris.

'Indeed,' said Dirk. He stepped into the darkness beyond and called out, 'Greetings, old man, it is I, Dirk the Magnificent!'

Silence met his words.

Dirk reached over and flicked the light switch. A dull glow from several ancient-looking lanterns fitted with modern bulbs filled the air with light.

The three adventurers walked into the main room of the cottage.

'Hellooo!' said Sooz.

Nothing.

'The Dark Lord visits, White One! Answer me!' bellowed Dirk. But all was silence. Dirk and Sooz exchanged a puzzled glance.

Something wasn't right.

'Hey, guys, look at this,' said Chris, picking up an envelope off the round oaken table in the middle of the room. 'It's addressed to you, Dirk.'

Dirk snatched it out of Chris's hands.

'Hey!' said Chris.

Dirk ignored him. The envelope had the words 'To His Imperial Dirkness' written in Hasdruban's flowing handwriting, each letter crafted with artistic precision. Dirk ripped it open and scanned the letter:

My dear fellow,

I'm afraid I'm in a bit of pickle. I'm locked up in these horrible dungeons below the Iron Tower by someone calling himself the Headmaster of Doom. He says he's the new Dark Lord! Oh my! But worst of all, I've just finished Agatha Marple's rather wonderful book DEATH ON THE GATWICK

EXPRESS. I would so much like to read the sequel, MASSACRE IN THE WENDLE VILLAGE TEA ROOMS. *I think I left it in my room. Could you get it to me somehow? There's a good boy.*

Dirk frowned and handed the letter back to Chris.

'Cripes, he's been kidnapped – by some sort of usurping impostor!' said Chris, before handing the letter over to Sooz. 'Calls himself the Headmaster of Doom. Why's that, do you think – as a counterpoint to the White Wizard being a Headmaster too?' said Chris.

'Some kind of Battle of the Headmasters?' said Sooz.

'Battle of the Headmasters? Perhaps so, although…' said Dirk, his voice trailing off.

'Yeah, it seems so improbable, doesn't it?' said Chris.

'Still, he's clearly been taken. Poor old Hasdruban, he's such a nice man!' said Sooz.

'Well, in any case, somehow Hasdruban managed to smuggle this letter out. Maybe Agrash helped him.'

'You'd think he'd have more concerns than just getting hold of the book he was reading,' said Chris.

'Actually, yes, good point. Maybe it's a coded message or something,' said Sooz.

'Well, he's a great fan of Agatha Marple. Loves detective novels. Told me once it was one of the main reasons he stayed on earth at all – that and his sense of love and duty towards the children of Whiteshields School, the sickening old fool!' said Dirk.

'Hey, come on, he's been really good to us!' said Sooz.

Dirk sighed. 'I suppose he has, yes, I have to admit. But still, I fear there is nothing in this letter but an old man's request for his favourite book.'

'Shouldn't we have a look around the house

anyway, just in case?' said Sooz. 'Either there's no secret message or we get the book for him anyway, just like he's asked.'

Dirk made a face. 'S'pose. Let's search the place, then.'

An hour later, Dirk, Chris and Sooz sat despondently at the oaken table. Around them, the cottage was a total mess, books and papers littered all over the place.

'There's just nothing here,' said Sooz, picking up Hasdruban's letter and giving it another once-over.

'Nothing, not a bean,' said Chris.

'No, indeed, not even a Blood Bean,' said Dirk.

'Blood Bean?' said Chris.

'Blood Beans. They grow only in the Deadlands. Used in various recipes by the Clans of the Undead,' said Dirk absently.

'Well, anyway, we've got to rescue him somehow, haven't we?' said Sooz.

'That old fool?' said Dirk. 'Pah...' He was about to say, 'Who cares? Let him rot!' but actually Dirk realised that wasn't really how he felt. In fact... Dirk sighed and said, 'Well... yes, I suppose. We should rescue him really, shouldn't we?'

'Yeah, but it's not going to be easy,' said Chris.

'In any case, and more importantly, I can't let this new Dark Lord take over, assuming he isn't just some petty chancer, so what choice do we have? I can't allow him to sit on my throne – it's my land, my tower. My armies of Goblins and Orcs, they're my toys...'

'Toys?' said Sooz.

'Errr...my people, I mean! My people, and I have to save them too,' said Dirk, hurriedly.

'Hmm...' said Sooz. 'Also, we have to think about what might happen if we don't do anything. With Hasdruban gone, they'd appoint a new White Wizard and he really might not be so easy to deal with!'

'Good point! There'd be war and everything, all over again!' said Dirk. 'We have to do it because it's the right thing to do… I mean…the practical thing! The practical, sensible, strategic, self-serving thing to do. Right?'

Chris and Sooz swapped a look, little smiles on their faces. Dirk raised an eyebrow. It was almost as if they believed he really did want to do it because it was 'right and good'. How could they think that? And what about his reputation?

He frowned darkly and snapped, 'What are you two grinning about?'

'Nothing. Nothing,' said Sooz airily. 'So how do we get there?' she added, changing the subject.

'Easy enough,' said Dirk with a shrug. 'We'll use a Magic Hole to travel to the Iron Tower. Hasdruban keeps several in his desk, I believe, so he can pop back and forth whenever he likes. With my Ring of Power, and me being me, i.e. the EVIL ONE!' He paused, narrowing his eyes and glancing between Sooz and Chris, as if challenging them to contradict him. But they said nothing. It seemed to Dirk that Sooz was trying to stifle a laugh. Or was she? Sometimes it was so hard to work out what these tricksy humans were really thinking!

'Well, anyway,' continued Dirk, 'I'll sort everything out, get rid of this dodgy Dark Lord. Set things back to normal.'

'OK... Sounds doable,' said Chris.

Dirk opened a drawer in Hasdruban's polished oak writing desk and pulled out what looked like a rolled-up strip of wallpaper.

'Here we go,' he muttered. He unfurled it and rolled it out across the wooden floor. It became... a hole – a black hole in the very fabric of time and space, a black hole into nothingness!

'You remember what to do?' said Dirk.

'Yup,' said Chris, 'we jump in and shout out the destination we want to go to.'

'Yes, but we have to be quick, as the Hole won't

hang around for ever. So, remember – we're off to the Iron Tower of Despair!'

With that, Dirk leaped into the Hole and shouted, 'The Iron Tower!' He landed on the blackness with a juddering thud, painfully jarring his knees.

Nothing happened.

Dirk frowned. He jumped up again, saying the words again. He landed with a thump, but again, nothing else happened.

'It's not working,' said Chris.

'Yeah, thanks, Chris, I would never have worked that out if you hadn't mentioned it,' said Dirk sarcastically.

'Well…it's not,' said Chris.

'Here, try this one,' said Sooz, pulling another out of the drawer. But that one didn't work either! None of the five Holes worked, in fact.

Dirk shook his head. 'It doesn't make sense,' he said. 'It's almost as if… But…surely not?'

'Almost as if what?' said Chris.

'Well, there's a spell in my library back home in the Iron Tower called the Impenetrable Seal of all the Planes – or the Hole Stuffer, as the Goblins call it. A spell that can shut off all the Magic Holes from working, to stop people using them to travel between the planes. But why would this usurper do that? Unless…'

'Unless what?' said Chris.

'He's scared of me! That's it. He doesn't want me returning to overthrow him, he wants to keep me out. By the Nine Hells!' said Dirk

'Or he's blocking the way because he's getting ready – preparing an army, or preparing a trap for you. Building up his strength,' said Sooz.

'Sounds more likely,' said Chris.

'Yeah, well. He's still scared of me, he must be. Who wouldn't be?' said Dirk.

Sooz and Chris looked Dirk up and down. He wore a T-shirt with a black skull on it over a pair of jeans, with black and red trainers on his feet. Dirk and Sooz exchanged another look.

'He may be scared of me, but he's not the chancer I thought he was.' said Dirk, hand on chin.

'What do you mean?' said Sooz.

'To cast that spell, the one that seals off the planes like that – that's not something an ordinary person could do. It requires serious power and, well, evil intent. Proper evil.'

'Ah,' said Sooz. 'So we'd better take him seriously, then.'

'Well, whatever his plans, perhaps we can throw a spanner in the works,' said Chris.

'A spanner? Into the works? I'm a Dark Lord, the nearest I'd ever get to a spanner is to command one of my Goblin minions to use one!'

'No, no, it's just an expression. It means to frustrate this bloke's plans. By getting there somehow, before he's ready, for instance,' said Chris.

'Easier said than done, but nevertheless my minions are giving good advice today,' said Dirk.

'We're your friends, Dirk, not your minions,' said Chris.

'Really? Oh… yes, I forgot. Sorry,' said Dirk.

'Actually, I think I might have the spanner we need, as it were. I know how we can get back there… Hasdruban told me,' said Chris.

No Good Deed Ever Goes Unpunished

'Oh, come on, Dirk, it's not that bad,' said Chris.

Dirk stood glumly outside the entrance of the shopping mall, holding out a tin cylinder labelled 'Whiteshields Church Youth Centre Charity Fund'. The skies were grey and a light rain fell upon him, just to round off his misery.

'Bah, have you any idea how this is going to affect my reputation?' said Dirk. 'I'm supposed to be the Dark Lord, the leader of the Darklands, commander of legions of Orcs and Goblins, purveyor of Evil Plans, feared by many, loved by none. Look at me! Trying to raise money to build some kind of youth centre for those wretched wormlings you humans call "children".'

'Loved by none? What about my mum? She loves you,' said Chris, laughing.

'Don't remind me!' said Dirk. Chris's mum, Dirk's foster mum, was always trying to give him a hug. She was also the local Reverend for Whiteshields Anglican Church, which was why they were here collecting for charity.

Well, that wasn't entirely true. Dirk was doing it for a different reason. Chris had got quite friendly with old Hasdruban, who'd become like an uncle or a mentor to him. Hasdruban told Chris about a back-up plan he'd had put in place when he first came to earth. It was a spell called

'Virtue's Journey'. Anyone from their world, trapped here on earth, could return home to the White Tower if they performed three Good Deeds and then recited the simple words, 'By Virtue's Power, take me to the Tower.' It would work for any denizen of the Commonwealth of Good Folk or the Darklands, hence the three Good Deeds requirement as a filter to keep out the bad guys. More importantly it didn't use the same magical system as the Magic Holes. It was new and unknown so the Seal of the Planes spell that the new Dark Lord had used wouldn't affect it. Theoretically.

But it wouldn't work for an earth native – the only way it would was if Dirk performed the three Good Deeds himself. Sooz and Chris loved that idea!

Dirk not so much.

So here he was, performing his first Good Deed. The White Tower wasn't the Iron Tower, but still it was the nearest he could get to the

Darklands for now, so that was the place to go. Last time he'd had to sneak in and out but this time it would be different, presumably, and they wouldn't just chuck him into a cell or put him on trial or something. Well, hopefully not, anyway. But first he had to perform three Good Deeds, and then keep it all secret for as long as possible. If his people back home in the Darklands found out that he was raising money for charity, he'd be a laughing stock!

And his first Good Deed wasn't going that well.

'I'm not getting many donations,' said Dirk. 'But I guess that's to be expected. I've never understood this charity thing anyway. Well, unless you were raising money to hire an army of mercenaries or to pay for an assassination or something…'

'Maybe you should stop smiling at them,' said Chris.

'What?' said Dirk. 'I thought you humans

liked people who smile?

'Yeah…not you so much, Dirk. Your smile is more…well, more of an Evil Grin. It frightens people.'

'Really?' said Dirk. 'Cool!'

As they talked, three young mothers approached, each wheeling a pushchair with a toddler strapped into it. As they drew near, Chris shook his collection box at them and said, 'We're collecting for the Youth Centre. Want to give something?'

'Ah, how lovely to see young boys like you doing their bit,' said one of the mothers, reaching for her purse. The others smiled and nodded approvingly.

'Why do you chain your worthless human spawn so?' said Dirk, gesturing at the babies fastened into their pushchairs. The mothers all froze for a moment in shock. Dirk frowned. Had he said something wrong?

'Ummm…he means…errr…' But not

even Chris could think of a positive way of spinning it.

Dirk realised then that he'd said something 'disturbing' and a little smile lifted the corner of his mouth. He couldn't help himself. He followed it up by giving them all the big grin.

The mothers recoiled with gasps of horror… and their children did too. The babies' faces became tiny masks of horror, mirrors of their mothers' – and then they began to wail. All three of them. Loudly.

Quickly the mothers hurried away, muttering things like 'Oh my,' and 'Worthless? How dare he?' and suchlike, whilst throwing furtive glances behind them. That made Dirk grin even more.

'Only you could make babies cry while collecting money for charity,' said Chris, shaking his head despairingly.

'I know, fantastic, isn't it?' said Dirk.

Chris gave him a long stare.

'Oh come on, I just smiled at them!'

'Well, don't! We've got that charity fun run later too – try not to ruin that!'

'Bah, running is never fun!' said Dirk. 'Well, unless you're running someone down, of course.'

The next day, Dirk and Chris were in Chris's room, playing a computer game. The game was called *Challenge of the Magi* and it featured duelling wizards. Behind them, Sooz was reading the local paper out loud to them. This is what it said:

The Wendle Herald

Oct 27th 2015

Community News

Local Kids Raise £1,200 for Local Hospice

Three kids from Whiteshields School have organised a Charity Fun Run through Willowdown Wood to raise money for the local hospice. Our correspondent, Delia Dimples, interviewed the three children.

Dirk Lloyd, the boy behind it all, said, 'I chose the hospice because it is a House of Death where people go to die. I mean, how cool is that? I thought…'

Dirk, an intense, serious boy, was interrupted in mid flow by his friend, Miss Susan Black.

'Yes, well, it's a place where those of us who are nearing the end of their lives go so that their last few days are

'Well,' said Sooz, 'can't say that interview went well!'

'Eh? Why? Sounds fine to me,' said Dirk.

Sooz rolled her eyes. 'Never mind,' she said.

'We raised a lot of money – more than we raised for the Youth Centre,' said Chris.

'The important thing is that they still count as Good Deeds, right?' said Dirk.

'Yup, so are you ready for the next one?' said Sooz.

---

comfortable and free of pain, where their loved ones can visit, knowing they are in good hands.'

The boy Dirk, who was a little strange, I have to tell you, then went on: 'Good place to visit if you're looking to raise an army of the undead too…' but then he was interrupted once more by Christopher Purejoie. 'Ahem! Yes… We may be children but we understand that everyone is mortal and we couldn't think of a better cause than the hospice.'

'What? I'm not mortal!' said the strange boy, before Susan and Christopher literally hustled him away and out of my sight.

The Fun Run was a great success and raised over £1,200 for the hospice. However, some runners complained of a boy in a Darth Vader mask holding a stick he claimed was a lightsaber and threatening the runners with it as they came past. 'Run faster, you wormlings, run!' he kept saying, apparently.

Dirk groaned. 'I suppose so. What is it?'

'A charity called Dream Maker,' said Sooz. 'Local charity for sick kids. Raising money to make their dreams come true.'

'What, the dreams of human children? What are they – free ice cream for all time? Meeting your favourite footballer? Singing with your favourite pop star? Bah, worthless dreams!'

'Oh, come on, these are children with awful diseases and stuff – they need every kindness they can get!' said Sooz.

'Well, fair enough, I guess, I just wish their dreams were more interesting. Now my dreams, they're something else. Launching a military coup and taking over Parliament! Having a massive statue built of myself as big as the Eiffel Tower, straddling London like a colossus! Sending a rocket to the moon and having my name tattooed on its face in massive letters of glowing steel so everyone can see it every night, up there in the sky! Or—'

'All right, all right, we get the picture,' said Sooz.

'So, what's the dream we have to make come true?' said Chris.

'Ummm…it's a little boy who… Well, he wants to meet Ricky Roony, his favourite Premier League football striker.'

'Hah, told you!' said Dirk.

Virtue's Journey

Sooz, Christopher and Dirk stood in a ring, holding hands. Chris and Sooz had backpacks with their favourite things in them like Chris's Chocolate Champions breakfast cereal, and Sooz's MP3 player. Dirk had nothing but his evil intellect. And his ring.

'So, are we ready, then?' said Dirk.

'I guess. Though I'm really not sure if what you did to that Ricky Roony counts as a Good Deed,' said Chris.

'He visited that kid, didn't he?' said Dirk.

'Made his dream come true?'

'Yeah, but what you call persuasion the police may well call something else…'

'Whatever,' said Dirk. 'The end justifies the means, right?'

'No, it doesn't, not when it comes to doing Good Deeds,' said Sooz.

'Really? Well… I guess we'll find out. Here we go!' said Dirk. 'I have completed three Good Deeds! By Virtue's Power, take me to the Tower!'

There was a flash and suddenly the three of them were standing on a white marble floor, inlaid with veins of turquoise blue. They were in the Entrance Hall of the White Tower! Around the edges of the vast, circular hall milled many people, queuing or remonstrating with the bureaucrats and officials of the Commonwealth of Good Folk who were sitting behind tables or in cubicles spread around the edges. This was where the daily administration of the Commonwealth of Good Folk went on. Several people nearby recoiled in surprise at the sight of them just appearing out of the blue.

A martial figure, dressed in white armour with a white shield and a sword at his side, addressed them.

'Who dares enter the hall using magic?' he demanded.

'That's a Paladin of the Whiteshields,' whispered Dirk to Sooz and Chris. 'Let me deal with him!'

'We have used the spell of Virtue's Journey to travel here,' he said to the Paladin, 'which means we're good guys, right?'

The Paladin frowned. 'Maybe,' he said. 'But aren't you…you know, Dirk, the Dark Lord, the Evil One, who has possessed the body of a human child?' The Paladin took a step forward, putting a hand on the hilt of his sword.

'Possessed, no! It was your own leader, Hasdruban, who gave me this form. And in any case, we are at peace, the Darklands and the

Commonwealth, aren't we?' said Dirk.

'We may be at peace, but that does not allow the Dark Lord himself to enter the Tower!' said the Paladin in increasingly heated tones. He began to draw his sword.

'Hold, Bashar!' cried a voice from behind.

Stepping through the crowd towards them was another figure in white armour. 'I will deal with this, my friend,' said the figure, and he lifted the visor on his helmet.

'Rufino!' said Sooz.

'Yes, my lady, welcome to the White Tower!" said the Paladin Rufino. Once Rufino had sworn allegiance to Sooz when she'd been the Moon Queen and ruler of the Darklands. Hasdruban had branded him a traitor for it, but that was before the peace, before things had changed so much. Now Rufino had been reinstated. He too travelled back and forth between earth and here, when he could. Dirk, Sooz and Christopher were like family to him now. He was also the drummer in Sooz's band.

'You know them?' said Bashar.

'I do, I can vouch for them,' said Rufino.

'But isn't that the Dark Lord himself, in child form?' said Bashar.

'It is. But fear not, I will take them to the White Council immediately,' said Rufino.

'Well, all right then,' said Bashar. 'I will come with you.'

Rufino nodded. 'Come, then.' He gestured for them all to follow. As they walked towards a pair of mighty oak doors, the entrance to the Council Chamber, Rufino and Sooz started to chat – about the latest song she'd written, 'Love Under the Dark Moon of Sorrows', and how she'd put in a drum solo for Rufino.

'Cool,' said Rufino. 'I've had some new drums made too, it's a unique sound. I'm calling it Medieval Drum 'n' Bass.'

'Great, can't wait to hear it, especially as I'm trying to create a new take on classic Goth

Rock with the song. A new type of drum might help…'

And so their conversation went. Bashar, who was sticking close to Dirk, looked down at him and frowned. 'What are they talking about?' he asked.

'Hah, don't ask me! These humans from earth are a crazy bunch, I can tell you. Makes you wish for the good old days when things were simple, doesn't it? Enemies, for all time, implacably sworn to destroy each other and so forth. No such thing as drum 'n' bass!'

Bashar nodded. 'Aye, true enough, no mucking about back then!'

'Now look at us. We're probably going to be allies. And Goth Rock has come to the White Tower.'

'The Rock Goth? Is that some kind of Stone Golem, raised up by evil magic?' said Bashar.

'Not so far from the truth, I reckon. But if I were you, I'd just forget about it,' said Dirk,

'Earth music – really, it's not worth trying to work it out.'

'Here we are,' said Rufino, and he rapped portentously on the great doors of the Council Chamber of the Commonwealth of Good Folk with the hilt of his sword.

A voice came from behind the doors.

'Who disturbs the council in their deliberations?'

'It is I, the Paladin Rufino. And I have the Dark Lord himself with me!'

'Which one?' said the voice.

'What?' said Rufino.

'Which one – is he a little Dark Lord or a big one? Answer the question!'

'Umm…' Rufino looked down at Dirk, who was beginning to look a little embarrassed.

'Err…the little one,' said Rufino.

'Well, that's a relief! Fine, come in,' said the voice and the great doors began to swing open.

'Bah, I'm the true Dark Lord, not that

wretched upstart, whoever he is. How dare they call me little!' muttered Dirk, clenching his fists and glowering angrily.

'There, there, my friend, said Rufino, patting Dirk on the back. 'I'm sure they're still scared of you, really.'

'Hey, you're the One and Only, Dirk, the One and Only, we know that!' said Chris soothingly. Dirk, always susceptible to a bit of flattery, unclenched his fists and stepped into the Council Chamber, a place he'd never expected to find himself in a thousand years. Well, not without being bound in chains first, anyway.

The floor was marble, with a long carpet of white and gold thread that led up to a great table of white wood around which sat twelve white-robed humans.

'Greetings, your Imperial Darkness,' said a woman with her hair bound up in a white gold circlet studded with blue gems. She had startling green eyes. 'I am Rosapina, the Chamberlain of the Tower, second in command only to Hasdruban himself. Your arrival is timely!'

Dirk stepped up to the table, flanked by his friends. 'So, you are aware of recent events?'

'Indeed, there is a new Evil One in the Tower, and he has somehow managed to kidnap our leader,' said Rosapina.

'Hah!' snorted a thin little fellow sitting next to her. 'Hardly difficult now that he's turned into a weakling milksop!'

'Now, now,' said an enormously fat lady on Rosapina's other side. 'We've been over this. Hasdruban is our rightful leader and that's that!'

'All very well, but the chances are Hasdruban is already dead, and we'll have to appoint a new White Wizard, someone who can fight a resurgent Darkness!' said the little fellow.

A hubbub of voices rose up around the table, all arguing at once. Dirk shook his head. If only he'd known how they ran things around here! He could have defeated this rabble a hundred times over.

'Silence!' bellowed Rosapina in a surprisingly powerful voice.

Everything went quiet.

'We do not know the nature of this new threat, this new Dark Lord, this new plague of black-hearted horror that blights the dreams of men and elves. Let us hope he is not so foully evil and degenerate as the last one…'

'Hey, right here!' said Dirk.

Rosapina hesitated. She nodded graciously at Dirk and went on. 'As evil as the previous Dark Lord before he became…enlightened.'

'Yeah, right,' said the angry little man seated beside her.

Dirk glared at him. He glared back.

'Anyway,' said Dirk, 'I'm still officially the Dark Lord!'

'That's not what our scouts are telling us. Goblins and Orcs march to the tower, swearing fearful oaths of allegiance to the new Lord of

Darkness… A great black fog belches up from the upper parapets of the tower to cover the sky in dark clouds. The borders have been sealed, our people who were brave enough to trade with the Darklands have been thrown out, their goods seized and the clothes literally torn from their backs, some of them subjected to some kind of new torture called "six of the best".'

'Six of the best? What the…?' said Dirk.

'Yes, and if they disobey they are threatened with 666 of the best!' said Rosapina.

'Wow, what's going on?' said Chris.

'We do not know any more,' said Rosapina. 'Our scouts cannot get near for they are spotted nearly every time. There are magical boxes on poles that track the movements of anyone who approaches them!'

Dirk frowned. 'Earth technology?'

'CCTV!' said Sooz.

'Wow, this is getting weirder,' said Chris.

'We think you can help us, your Imperial

Dirkness,' said Rosapina. 'With your inside knowledge, perhaps you can sneak into the Darklands, find out who this new Dark Lord really is, what he wants, what his weaknesses are, if he has any, and what he has done with Hasdruban.'

'Well, he sent me a letter, did Hasdruban,' said Dirk.

'What?' said the angry man. 'A letter to you, and not to us, his High Council?'

'Indeed,' said Dirk. 'Hasdruban and I are... friends. Sort of. Anyway, he is still alive, although imprisoned in the Dungeons of Doom.'

'The Dungeons of Doom? How awful!' said Rosapina.

'Don't worry about it! I'm not going to sneak in – I'm going to blast my way in with my Ring of Power. I'll blast this impostor off my throne and out of my tower, and send him on his way with his tail between his legs like the stinking dog that he is, whoever he is, and I'll bring

Hasdruban back with me!'

With that, Dirk held up his hand with the Great Ring of Power on it, the Great Ring whose runes coruscated with flaming fire, burning with magical energy, the Great Ring that could unleash mighty bolts of ravening force against his enemies!

Various White Councillors recoiled in horror, muttering and flinching, for the Great Ring had been their nemesis for hundreds of years.

Except that the Great Ring wasn't writhing with flaming runes or humming with energy like it usually did when it was in the Darklands. It was as quiet and as boring as it was when it was back on earth – just a simple band of metal.

Dirk lowered the ring and stared at it. What was going on?

'It seems your Great Ring has lost its power,' said Rosapina.

'Get him!' yelled the little man, jumping up.

'Yes,' chorused several others, leaping up too.

There was a chorus of voices saying stuff like 'Get him whilst we've got the chance!', 'Kick him when he's down!' or 'Don't look a gift horse in the mouth!' and so on.

Several of the Paladins that lined the walls of the chamber moved forward, reaching for their swords. Dirk stepped back, his eyes widening in surprise. Rufino, Sooz and Chris, though, stepped up to protect him. Thank the Nether Gods for friends, Dirk thought to himself.

'GET A HOLD OF YOURSELVES, YOU FOOLS!' yelled Rosapina at the top of her voice. Everyone froze.

'Can't you see? He's just a boy, a weak, pitiful human boy. What are we, child murderers now?' continued Rosapina.

Sheepishly, the councillors shuffled their feet, avoiding Rosapina's gaze.

Dirk frowned. Weak, pitiful human boy? Is that really how I look to them? he thought.

'Look at him, he's not our enemy any more!'

said Rosapina. Those councillors that had risen to their feet sat quietly down. The Paladins stood back.

Now that he wasn't in imminent danger of being torn to pieces, Dirk turned his attention to his ring. He rubbed it, caressed it. Spoke to it. But the ring was dead. Inert. Powerless. Dirk blinked up at the chamberlain, his face reddening with embarrassment again. She's right, he thought to himself, that's all I am now, a wretched kid, a hopeless human child. His days of dark glory were over.

'Actually, that's not true, he's not weak,' said Sooz. 'He isn't just an ordinary boy. He's brilliant, he's a genius! He could outwit any one of you.'

Dirk stared at her, jaws agape.

'Yup,' said Chris. 'He's done the most incredible things since he's been Dirk, and hardly any of them with the Ring.'

'Indeed, I can vouch for the truth of this, my

lady,' said Rufino. 'He is courageous, intelligent, resourceful and cunning, and would make for a formidable enemy even as he is, as a small boy.'

Dirk's heart swelled with pride. At last, the recognition he deserved!

Rosapina narrowed her eyes. 'But can he be trusted?'

Rufino, Chris and Sooz exchanged looks.

'Ah, well…' stammered Rufino.

'Ummm…let's see now…' flannelled Sooz.

'Trust, hmm…well, it depends on how you define trust,' muttered Chris.

'Hey! Hey, right here!' said Dirk.

Rosapina folded her arms.

Rufino put a hand up. 'Actually, that's the wrong question to ask, my lady. What I can say is that he is no longer truly Evil and once he has set himself a task he will never give up until it is completed or he has been destroyed. And I will swear to that on my oath as a Paladin!'

Rosapina nodded slowly. 'All right. Dirk still

knows the Darklands, right? He's our best bet to get in there, to find out the nature of this new threat, yes?'

Rufino looked over at Dirk, who nodded, vigorously. 'Agreed, yes,' said Rufino to Rosapina.

'Well, then, you and your friends will go to the Darklands and find out what's what. Agreed?' she said.

Rufino looked at Dirk, Sooz and Chris. 'Agreed?' he said.

'Agreed!' they said.

Scout and About

Rufino, Dirk, Chris and Sooz were gearing themselves up in the armoury of the White Tower. Well, the others were. Dirk was staring at the Great Ring.

'You're sure you didn't swap it with a fake version or something, like last time?' said Dirk.

'NO!' said Sooz and Chris together.

'For the hundredth time,' added Sooz, 'that's the real one.'

'It certainly looks like it. But that means…' Dirk's words trailed off despairingly.

'What does it mean?' asked Rufino.

'That means this usurper, the new Dark Lord… He must have sucked all the power out of it.'

'How would he do that?' said Chris.

'By being truly the Evil One. By being the rightful Dark Lord,' said Dirk

'Ah… I see,' said Sooz, putting a comforting hand on Dirk's shoulder.

'Which makes you…?' said Chris.

'It makes me Dirk Lloyd, a kid from earth. A nobody,' said Dirk. 'I'm not even the official Dark Lord any more!'

Sooz frowned in thought. 'Someone's stolen that from you,' she said to Dirk, trying to raise his spirits. 'Isn't it time you took back what's yours?'

Dirk stared at her. 'You're right. Of course you are! I'll fight this, fight it until the end, I'll never give up. I'm the rightful Dark Lord after all! I created the Darklands! I built the Goblin

Warrens, the Dungeons of Doom. I fought the do-gooding fools of the Commonwealth to a standstill; it was I that almost conquered the world! I! I built the Iron Tower, built it with my own hands from nothing…'

'I thought Gargon built it?' said Chris.

'Well, yes, technically. But I gave the orders, right?' said Dirk, distracted from his rant.

'But you didn't actually build it with your own hands, though,' said Chris.

'Oh, come on, every great endeavour needs a planner, a visionary – the rest is just grunt work!'

'Yeah, but still, Gargon actually did the work, right? I can remember him complaining about it,' continued Chris.

'Gargon's a great minion, but he'd be nothing without me!' said Dirk

'Hold on, where is old Gargy, anyway?' said Rufino.

Chris, Sooz and Dirk exchanged glances.

'Good question,' said Sooz.

'Wasn't he supposed to be playing in your band this weekend, Sooz?' asked Chris.

'Yes, but last I heard he was in the Darklands, visiting. He said he'd be back in time for the concert, though,' said Sooz.

'But you haven't heard from him? Hmm, let's see. This "Headmaster of Doom", he's got Hasdruban. Almost certainly Agrash as well, from what I can tell, so he's probably got Gargon locked up too!' said Dirk.

'Blimey, that's like half our band. Who is this guy?' said Sooz.

'Time to find out,' said Rufino. 'Let's go.'

'Hold on – where, though? There's no point just marching up to the border, we'll just get spotted if there are CCTV cameras all over the place,' said Christopher.

'Don't worry about that, I know all the secret passages in and out of the Darklands,' said Dirk. 'I built most of them!'

'What, you actually built them?' said Chris.

'Oh, all right, my Goblin engineers did, but I gave the orders, right?'

'Just checking,' said Chris.

'So, where to, then?' said Rufino.

'There's a hidden trail that leads up to some hills on the edge of the Borderlands. There we can find a tunnel system that'll lead us to the foothills overlooking the Plains of Desolation. If this new Dark Lord is training up an army, that's where we'll find them, camped out on the plains,' explained Dirk.

'Right, we'll wait until dusk – you lead the way,' said Rufino.

Dirk and his minions – or so he liked to think of Chris, Sooz and Rufino – emerged from a small cave opening in the foothills of the Grey Scarps, a range of hills to the southwest of the Plains of Desolation.

Up ahead was a low ridge. They clambered

their way up over pale grey rocks jutting up like islands out of a river of green grass that flowed across the hills. Rufino was the first to pop his head up over the top of the ridge and promptly ducked back down again.

'A camp! A BIG camp,' he warned. 'Slowly now, stick your heads up and take a look.'

Gingerly, they peeked over the top of the ridge. It overlooked the edge of a huge encampment. Nearby were some tarpaulin shelters – primitive one-sided tents, basically.

'Orc bivouac!' muttered Dirk.

And indeed, big hairy Orcs were wandering around all over the place, fixing armour, cooking up rations, itching and farting, arguing and mucking about, just like Orcs do.

They were also polishing swords and stuff.

'Wait a minute,' said Dirk. 'Those swords, look at them.'

'They look like rulers!' said Sooz.

'Sharp, though.'

'And what are those,' said Rufino, 'on their belts?'

'Catapults! Old-fashioned schoolboy catapults,' said Chris.

'They look powerful, though – deadly at close range, I would think,' said Dirk.

'And their helmets! They look like… They're not helmets at all, they're caps. School caps,' said Sooz.

'It's like an army from an old-fashioned public school!' said Chris.

Rufino looked at Dirk questioningly. Dirk shrugged. 'Calls himself the Headmaster of Doom; I guess it's all part of that,' he said.

'Wait a minute, what's all that over there?' said Chris, pointing beyond the Orc bivouac.

Dirk could see rows of canvas tents, more advanced than the Orcish shelters. 'Goblin camp,' said Dirk. 'They're more intelligent than the Orcs, but not as good in a fight.'

'No, beyond them even,' said Chris.

They all raised their eyes. At the far end of the encampment they could see many large black pavilion tents. Most of them appeared to be made of canvas, but some had banners fluttering above them and these looked like they were made of velvet.

'That's not good,' said Dirk.

'Why?' said Rufino.

'Whoever – or whatever – is camping out in them… Well, they're not going to be Orcs or Goblins,' said Dirk.

'So?' said Chris.

'I suspect they're much worse!' said Dirk.

'Hold on, what's that?' said Sooz. 'Isn't that the…?'

'The Midnight Chariot, yes it is!' said Dirk.

From the east a column of troops was marching through the camp. At the front was a great chariot of black steel, pulled by two huge black horses – NightMares, bred by the Master of the Steeds of Doom in the Dark Stables of the

Iron Tower to serve the Dark Lord. And there he was, riding in the chariot. The usurper. The upstart. The new Dark Lord. Twelve feet tall, covered in a raggedy black cloak with a large, black mortarboard on his head. In one hand he held a long, black cane of some kind.

The four heroes (well, three heroes and Dirk) stared hard, trying to make out his face as he drew near.

'It's Grousammer!' said Sooz.

'No way!' said Dirk.

'Yes way, dude,' said Sooz.

'Grousammer? Who is Grousammer?' said Rufino.

'He's the old Headmaster of Whiteshields School, before… Well…' said Sooz, glancing at Dirk.

'Before Dirk shaved off his beard and got rid of him,' said Chris.

Dirk couldn't help himself – he smirked at the memory.

'Shaved off his…?' said Rufino, confused.

'It's a long story,[2]' said Sooz. 'Anyway, it seems he's back, and somehow…he's the new Dark Lord!'

'Oh my!' said Chris, putting a hand up to his mouth. 'He must have found the Essence of Evil and drunk it all up!'

'What? You were supposed to get rid of it!' said Dirk

'I was, I was, but I couldn't find it anywhere!' said Chris.

'Oh, so now you tell us!' said Dirk.

'I didn't want to worry you, maybe even set you off on a quest to find it – you know how you're drawn to it. You might have found it and swallowed it, turned proper evil again,' said Chris.

'Well, anyway, it seems this Hammer of the Grouse has found it,' said Rufino.

---

[2] As told in the first book in the Dark Lord series, Dark Lord: The Teenage Years. You'd better read it, if you haven't already, or be thrown into the Black Pit of a Thousand Lines.

'And drunk deeply of it!' said Dirk.

'That explains all the crazy headmaster stuff then,' said Chris.

'That's true,' said Sooz. 'But I think we have to be careful not to underestimate him – Grousammer didn't exactly start off as a decent kind of guy. He was embezzling money from the school when he was a real headmaster, for a start.'

'Right, so there's no telling how far to the Dark side the Essence will take him,' said Chris.

'So, a superevil, mad Dark Lord who believes in old-style public school teaching?' surmised Sooz.

'Yup, that's about the size of it,' said Chris.

'At least we know what we're up against,' said Rufino.

'Hold on,' said Dirk. 'What's that coming up behind the chariot?'

Several large carts pulled by mules and carrying barrels were following on behind.

'Looks like supplies?' said Rufino.

As the carts came by, they began to turn, heading for the black pavilions in the distance. Unnoticed, a barrel fell off the back of one of the carts, and rolled up to the base of the ridge, right below them. The lid cracked open, and out tumbled a stream of grain or pellets of some kind.

'I need to see some of those,' said Dirk.

'Why?' said Chris.

'If they are what I think they are, we could be in serious trouble. We need to find out.'

'I'll go,' said Rufino.

'No, you're too big and noticeable, I'll go,' said Sooz, and off she crawled. Rufino tried to grab her but she was too fast. Chris wanted to call her back, but that would have given them away. They had no choice but to watch, hearts in their mouths, as she set off on her own. But they needn't have worried. Carefully, she inched her way down the side of the hill, grabbed a handful of the pellets and crawled her way back up again.

'You are brave, my lady,' said Rufino.

'Actually, she looks half Goblin anyway, so she's perfectly disguised,' joked Chris.

'Oh, very funny,' said a dust-covered Sooz, as she handed over the pellets to Dirk.

'Here you go, your Dirkness!'

'Thanks,' said Dirk absently as he examined the pellets. Then he sighed. 'It is as I feared. They're Blood Beans.'

'Those beans that grow in the Deadlands? What's wrong with them?' said Chris.

'Blood Beans are rations for an army,' said Dirk.

'Yeah, so?'

'An army of the undead…' said Dirk.

The Face of Evil

Rufino, Chris, Sooz and Dirk were sitting in a little lobby area at the top of the White Tower where people waited to see the White Wizard or his chamberlain. Dave the Storm Crow had also turned up to be with Dirk, travelling from earth – he could still travel between the planes, unaffected by the Headmaster of Doom's great spell. Shelves around the lobby were lined with books. Dave stood on top of one of them and squawked. Dirk noticed the book was called

How to Lead a Life of Blameless Purity.

Pah, do-gooding nonsense, thought Dirk. He looked up at Dave and raised an eyebrow. Dave squawked and cocked a leg over the book…

'Heh, heh,' sniggered Dirk.

Around the rest of the room were low tables with big fluffy white cushions scattered about for the comfort of those waiting in the lobby. Magically powered silver samovars floated in the air, ready to dispense hot tea on demand. Each low table had a magic biscuit tin that never ran out.

A big fire kept it warm and cosy. Elvish choral music played in the background. It was nice – sickeningly nice.

On one side there was a big, white door covered in strange runes – the door to the White Wizard's Inner Sanctum. A large carved face had been set into the door. It looked a bit like Dirk's Dark Lord Seal, in fact, the eyes and tusks picked out in gold. It was called the Face of Evil.

It looked like that because it was a perpetual reminder of what the office of the wizard was for – defeating the Dark Lord and all his works. It was also a lock.

You had to know the magic word or the code to get that magical mask to open the door, and only the White Wizard knew that, so for now it remained resolutely shut.

Opposite was another door, with a sign on it that said 'Chamber of the Chamberlain' – Rosapina's office, basically. The four of them were waiting to go in and tell the chamberlain what they'd discovered on their scouting trip.

Dirk pondered the situation. Clearly Grousammer was aiming at conquering the Commonwealth. He was amassing a big army – OK, not that much of a problem. Dirk himself had done that several times and never managed to overwhelm the armies of Good entirely. On the other hand, Dirk had never managed to bring the Clans of the Undead into the equation.

Sure, he'd tried in the past, had even had some success. He'd once had a company of Vampires riding on NightMares before they'd been destroyed in the Battle of the Night Made Day, hundreds of years ago. But he could never build a true alliance with the Clans of the Undead, for they were never interested in what he had to offer them. They weren't afraid of him and they didn't want land or power. In fact, he never could work out what they did want – which was a shame, because they'd make great allies. They had vampire lords, regiments of ghouls and hordes of zombies. Those zombies could be replenished after every battle too, whether you won or lost.

But Grousammer had managed it. All those black pavilions, so useful for keeping the sun off your back, proved it. This included black velvet pavilions – and those were reserved only for the lords of the dead: the vampires. It wasn't just a few of them, either, judging by the number of Blood Beans he was delivering to feed them. And you had to feed them regularly – otherwise they'd turn on your other living troops, for the Clans of the Undead didn't really differentiate between Orc and human, Goblin or Elf. They were all blood and brains to them. Well, except that Elves and humans tasted better.

Absently, Dirk reached for a book on a nearby table. He drummed his fingers on the cover. What had Grousammer promised them? Whatever it was, it had to be big!

Dirk glanced at the book. Hold on a second! It was a copy of Agatha Marple's *Massacre in the*

Wendle Village Tea Rooms, the book Hasdruban had mentioned in the letter to Dirk they'd found in the White Wizard's house back on earth.

'Well, well, who would have thought it,' he muttered to himself as he opened it. Someone had written something on the inside cover – clearly Hasdruban himself, judging by the perfectly drawn letters.

An Eye for an Eye and a Tooth for a Tooth
That is the way forward
Hasdruban the White

That sounds like the old fire and brimstone Hasdruban, not the kindly old fellow he is now, thought Dirk to himself. Unless…was this a clue? His eyes flicked over to the stylised Face of Evil on the door. His thoughts were suddenly interrupted as the door to the Chamber of the Chamberlain opened and out stepped Rosapina.

'So sorry to keep you waiting,' she said. 'Come

in, come in, I'm eager to hear your report. There is much to discuss!'

Everyone got up and headed over to her chamber, but Dirk lingered a little. He went over to the other door and examined the Face. Behind him, the chamber door closed – they hadn't noticed he wasn't with them. Yet. Dave the Storm Crow hopped down from the bookshelf and started pecking at the biscuits from the never-ending biscuit tin.

'Hey, get out of there!' said Dirk, but the bird just squawked dismissively, as if to say, 'Go away – these biscuits are too good.' Dirk sighed. Whatever. He had more important things to worry about. He turned his attention back to the door.

The face was quite beautiful, in fact, just like his own seal was. Well, his seal was beautiful to him, he supposed. To others it probably just looked like a snarling, hideous demon. Interestingly, bits of the mask were picked out in gold lacquer

– the eyes and the two front teeth, tusks really, that rose up from behind the bottom lip. Dirk gingerly pushed one of the golden eyes – it sank into the mask with a click! He pushed the other, and it did the same, so he tried the fangs – click, click!

The mask whirred and rattled for a few seconds, and then rotated suddenly and the door swung open.

'Excellent!' said Dirk. He had to suppress the urge to let out one of his Evil Laughs. He stepped into the Inner Sanctum of the White Wizard, a place he had only ever dreamed of entering – and even then it would have been with fire and steel, either as a conqueror or a prisoner. Who would have thought after all those years of war that one day he would just walk in, effectively at the invitation of the White Wizard himself?

Inside he found a circular study with a big white oak table in the middle and a large comfy chair behind it. Around the walls were plaques and trophies, mostly depicting great battles and victories over Dirk and his armies.

Bah, none of their defeats, though, I see, no pictures of all those other White Wizards before him that I crushed, for instance. Typical! thought Dirk to himself.

The table itself was bare, except for two things – a small box, and a little phial of liquid that glowed with a bright, white, ultraviolet light.

Dirk picked up the phial of liquid, and examined it. 'Essence of Good', it said on the label. Essence of Good! Anyone who drank the Essence of Evil became a Dark Lord – anyone drinking this would become a supergood White Wizard, he supposed…

Or maybe a fanatical do-gooder, prepared to kill, like Hasdruban had once been. It was a two-edged sword.

Dirk opened up the box – there were two Anathema Crystals inside. Smashing one on the floor would teleport everyone nearby either to earth or the Darklands, depending on where you started. And it would also strip out all the Essence of Evil (or Good) that anyone might have inside them.

That Hasdruban. Not so stupid after all. He'd known they'd need a powerful White Wizard to counter Grousammer. And whoever drank the Essence of Good would become that White Wizard. It'd be just like that game of duelling wizards Dirk and Christopher had played. What was it called? *Challenge of the Magi*, that was it. And once they'd defeated the Dark Headmaster, they could use the crystal to return to normal. Except most people didn't want to return to normal once they'd become a Dark Lord – and no doubt the same was true once you'd been a White Wizard.

Dirk had to admit, all things being equal, that if you were only going to have one of them, it'd be preferable to have the White Wizard rather than the Dark Lord. Still… He made a face.

It might be safer, just having a wizard, but it wouldn't be nearly as much fun!

Anyway. The plan was sound. Good old Hasdruban! Dirk would become the White Wizard, fight a magical duel with the Dark Lord, and win. After all, Dirk knew all the dark tricks, he knew what Grousammer would be thinking, he could outwit him. Sure, it'd be weird for a while being a White Wizard but once it was done, he'd use the crystal to revert to normal. (Well, revert to being a human child. He supposed you couldn't really call Dirk 'normal' at the best of times.)

Dirk frowned. But did he really want to be a White Wizard? He'd turn into a wishy-washy do-gooder, helping people out and being nice and kind. How boring!

Needs must, however. Bullets must be bitten, as the humans say.

Dirk held the phial of glowing white liquid up to his mouth and... hesitated.

He'd become pure good…

'No way!' said Dirk out loud. 'I'm the Dark Lord, THE Dark Lord, the first, the best…I can't do this!'

He blinked. He tried again, lifting up the phial almost to his lips, but to no avail. He shook his head. 'It's no good, I just can't do it.'

Dirk lowered the phial and sighed.

Wait a minute… thought Dirk to himself, his hand coming up to his chin, his brow furrowing in evil thought. Someone else as the White Wizard… Hmm… A White Wizard, a Dark Lord and a big duel, and him with an Anathema Crystal. All he had to do was to get them together, face to face. Dirk could use the crystal, send them both to earth where they'd lose their Essences, the wizard would return to normal, the Dark Lord would become that sneaky wretch Grousammer, a rather vulgar failed headmaster, and Dirk could take back what was his. Brilliant!

All right, then, if not him, then who?

'Christopher, oh, CHRISTOPHER!' shouted Dirk at the top of his voice.

'Yes, what is it? said Chris, a few moments later, coming up to the door. Behind him were Sooz and Rufino.

'How'd you get in here?' said Sooz.

'Evil genius,' said Dirk with a matter-of-fact shrug.

Sooz raised her eyes.

'Rosapina wants to talk to you,' said Rufino.

'In a minute. Now, how would you like to be a mighty White Wizard, Christopher?'

'You want to play *Challenge of the Magi*? Here? Right now?' said Christopher, puzzled.

'No, no, not a wizard in a game, in real life,' said Dirk.

'What? What are you on about this time, you deranged despot?' said Christopher.

Dirk held up the glowing phial of white liquid. He could feel its effects even now – bizarrely he felt like giving Christopher a great big hug for calling him a despot[3]. And even stranger, he didn't want to stretch him out on the Racks of Pain for calling him deranged!

By the Nine Hells, he thought to himself, thank the Dark Gods that Mrs Purejoie isn't here – I'd call her Mum, and hug her too! This stuff is dangerous!

'Well?' said Chris.

'This,' said Dirk, pointing to the phial, 'is Essence of Pure Good. Just like the Essence of Pure Evil, but, you know…Good, instead.'

'Like that black evil goo that turned you back into the Dark Lord? That turned Sooz into the Vampire Queen?' said Christopher, a worried look on his face.

'Indeed,' said Dirk. 'You made such a beautifully perfect Vampire Queen, didn't you, Sooz!'

Sooz smiled weakly,

---

[3] DESPOT: A ruler with absolute power. A person who wields power oppressively, a tyrant.

'Errr… No, I don't think so!' said Chris. 'She wanted to drink our blood!'

Sooz made a face, and muttered, 'Sorry!' under her breath.

'Well, you can't have everything, can you?' said Dirk

Chris raised his eyes. 'Whatever,' he said. 'Anyway, this white goo, what will that do?'

'Turn you into the White Wizard!' said Dirk.

Chris stared at Dirk.

'And you want me to drink it?' said Chris.

'Yes! You'd make a great White Wizard. You're pretty decent and sickeningly good already – you'd become a mighty Wizard! And then you could take on this new Dark Lord, whoever he is.'

'What? No way! I'm a kid, I'm not a White Wizard. I don't want to be a White Wizard, not after seeing what happened to Sooz!'

'But you did so well in *Challenge of the Magi*, you almost beat me, the only time you've ever come close to beating me in a game, ever!'

'That's a computer game! It's not real. And even if I did somehow beat this Dark Lord, what then? How do I get back to normal?'

'Don't worry, that's not a problem, we'd use one of those Anathema Crystals. Anyway, you might not want to return to normal, you might enjoy being a White Wizard – spells at your fingertips, armies of Paladins and Elves to command, the respect of all the so-called Good Folk.'

Christopher folded his arms. 'That sounds great – in a game! I mean, I don't want to be a Wizard in real life, right. I just want...well, to be me. I'd miss my mum and dad for a start! Anyway, what if I ended up like the old Hasdruban – a fanatical, murdering nutter?' he said.

'Come on, Chris, you couldn't be like that, I'm sure of it. It's your turn to be a hero! You'll be loved and worshipped...'

Chris shook his head. 'How can you be so

sure? No, I'm sorry, Dirk, but you're forgetting – I'm just a kid from earth, I'm still at school! I don't want to be turned into a Wizard, I don't know anything about armies of Paladins and stuff. It's…it's just too much, it's too scary!'

Dirk stared at him in irritation. He shook the phial in Chris's face.

'You'd better do as I say, minion, or I'll…'

'What?' said Chris. 'You'll do what? You're Dirk now, you're not the Dark Lord, you can't even use the ring any more. And anyway, you won't admit it but we both know you'd never actually hurt me, even if you could, would you?'

Dirk blinked. By the Nine Hells, Chris was right. And it wasn't just because he was holding Essence of Good in his hand. He put his hand up to his chin.

Hmm.

It was clear he was going to have to try something else…

Breakfast of Champions

Dirk, Sooz, Chris and Rufino were sitting together at breakfast in the refectory of the White Tower. Elsewhere, Paladins, soldiers, priests, officials and so on were all at breakfast too.

'It's difficult,' said Rufino. 'Rosapina thinks they can hold out for a while, but if the Headmaster of Doom has an alliance with the Clans of the Undead…' Rufino shook his head. 'The armies of the Commonwealth cannot hold out against such menace for ever!'

'We need to chop off the head of the snake,' said Dirk.

'Indeed,' said Rufino, 'but how do we get to him?'

'A magical duel of wizards!' said Dirk, glancing at Chris. Chris looked uncomfortable.

'Can't you see that what you're asking is just too much?' said Sooz. 'I mean, Chris is just an ordinary earth kid, he can't be a White Wizard. It's simply not fair!'

'Not to mention what would happen if Chris actually lost. Have you considered that?' said Rufino.

Dirk blinked in surprise. Actually, he hadn't considered that. Chris could get killed! He looked over at Chris, and then down at Chris's cereal bowl, full of Chocolate Champions he'd brought all the way from earth. But then another thought came to him.

'Hah, don't be silly, he'd have me at his back

– me and my evil genius! He can't possibly lose.'

'How can you be so sure?' said Rufino.

'Remember, I'm a Dark Lord too. I *was* the Essence of Evil. I know how Grousammer thinks, I know what's driving him and what his weaknesses are. That'll give us the edge,' said Dirk.

'Perhaps,' said Rufino.

'Still, it's a risk – a big risk to ask a boy to take,' said Sooz. 'Why not me?'

'No, no,' said Dirk. 'You were the Moon Queen once, the Mistress of the Iron Tower of Despair, the Dark Lady. The Essence of Good won't be so effective on you. Chris, though, he's so thoroughly – sickeningly, even – decent that he will make a truly great White Wizard!'

'I'm sorry, but the thought of turning into the White Wizard just terrifies me. I want to be me, is that so wrong?' said Chris, taking a spoonful of milk-soaked Chocolate Champions.

Dirk's eyes gleamed as he followed Chris's

hand to and from his cereal.

'Of course, I understand,' said Dirk.

Suddenly Chris spat his food out. 'Aarrrrggghhh!' howled Chris, leaping to his feet. His eyes began to water and his hand went to his throat, trying to ease the pain that wracked his mouth and tongue!

'What's the matter, Chris?' said Sooz.

'He's been poisoned!' yelled Rufino.

'Argh, someone's put chillies in my breakfast! Water, anyone, please, water!' rasped Chris.

'Here you are,' said Dirk, handing Chris a mug. Quickly Chris downed the contents.

Nobody noticed that the contents glowed with an ultraviolet light…

'That's better,' said Chris, blinking. And then he gasped.

'Wha—' was all he could get out as he began to shudder and shiver and shake. He began to change shape. He started growing! Up, and up – so tall! His eyes changed to the purest blue, filled entirely with blueness until they began to glow with aquamarine energy, and his hair grew long and lush and very, very silver. Long white robes formed around him, his skin turning as white as marble with a silvery sheen, like some kind of alabaster saint.

'Dirk, what have you done?' said Rufino.

'I gave him the Essence of Good,' said Dirk, with a big grin.

'How could you be so beastly?' said Sooz.

Dirk looked at her and shrugged a 'what do you expect' shrug.

Sooz glared back at him. 'Oooh, you little…'

Around them, the rest of the breakfasting Good Folk rose up from their seats in surprise. Chris reared up before them, nearly ten feet tall, looking…well, looking like an angel – a wingless angel.

He looked down at Dirk and said, in a voice like a silver bell, 'You tricked me!'

'And your point is?' replied Dirk, still grinning.

'But you called me friend; how could you do this to me?'

'True, true, but I'm betting that now you're utterly good, you won't want revenge,' said Dirk.

'Revenge? No, you're right, revenge is a pointless emotion, it corrupts the soul,' said Chris.

'You will be the new White Wizard, the champion of the Good Folk,' said Dirk.

'You shouldn't have done that, Dirk,' said Rufino. 'Christopher! Are you there? What shall we do? Do you want us to change you back?'

The White Wizard Christopher paused. A look of saintly calm descended over his features.

'No…' he said. 'No, I don't think so. I am at peace,' he said.

'At peace?' said Dirk, a little worriedly.

'I am at one with everything. All is love!' said Christopher, smiling beatifically.

'What? What about the Dark Lord? Don't you want to smite him, punish the evil that he is, destroy his foul works for ever?' said Dirk.

'Destroy? No, never destroy,' said Chris dreamily.

Dirk noticed that Sooz and Rufino and many others were looking up at Chris, looking up at him with happiness on their faces too. Christopher was literally radiating an aura of love and peace and it was beginning to affect those around him.

Not Dirk, though, obviously.

'Hey,' said Dirk. 'We need you to lead the armies of the Commonwealth against the Headmaster of Doom! We need you to be a White Wizard at war!'

Chris looked down at Dirk. 'I'm sorry, Dirk, but don't you see? Violence is wrong.'

'Uh-huh, and what are we going to do when he comes to kill us all with an army of the undead?' says Dirk.

'I shall reason with him,' said Angel Chris.

'He's a *headmaster*, Christopher! Since when

have they listened to reason?'

'It doesn't matter, Dirk, all that is an illusion,' said Christopher, who then sat and folded his legs into the lotus position, holding his arms out to either side. He closed his eyes – and began to float.

Around him, all was love and peace…

Dirk put his hands on his hips and stared. This wasn't quite working out how he'd planned!

Kidnapped!

'You have to help me, Susan Black!' said Dirk angrily.

Sooz and Dirk were sitting in the White Wizard's Inner Sanctum, Dirk in the wizard's chair, Sooz perched on the edge of his massive oaken desk. They were having an argument – a big argument.

'I won't help you lie to Christopher like that, it's not right!' retorted Sooz. 'You've already tricked him once!'

'But he's not going to do anything if we don't.

He's just going to sit there spreading peace and love around like so much manure!' said Dirk. 'Holy manure, but manure nonetheless.'

'What's wrong with that? This world could do with it!' said Sooz.

'He has to lead us in battle against the Headmaster of Doom, don't you see? It's the only way we can defeat him, and restore me to the throne.'

'So you want me to pretend to Chris that Grousammer has kidnapped his mum, just so you can sit on the Throne of Skulls once more, is that it?'

'Well, yes, exactly… NO, no, I mean, so we can save the Commonwealth and the Darklands. Rescue whatshisname… So we…umm…we can have peace!' said Dirk.

'Oh, please, you're sounding ridiculous now,' said Sooz.

'But there's no other way! He won't listen to reason, he's off "being at one with the universe", whatever that means. Off with the fairies, more like!'

Sooz shook her head. 'First of all, you play an awful trick on Chris, and turn him into something he doesn't want to be. Then when it turns out you can't manipulate him in the way you want to, you decide to make up a horrible story about his mum being kidnapped and threatened with death, just to get him to do what you want, to get what you need done!'

'Yes. And your point is?'

Sooz sighed. 'The point, Dirk, is that you should be doing everything in your power to get Christopher back to normal!'

'I am! It's just that he has to have a duel with Grousammer first,' said Dirk.

'Well, I'm not going to get involved in that, all right? I'm not going to be party to such a monstrous lie, and that's that!' said Sooz, huffily crossing her arms. 'In fact, if you so much as mention to him that his mum has been kidnapped, I'll tell him the truth, that it's all one big lie, made up by his so-called friend – you!'

Dirk glowered. 'I see,' he said, menacingly.

'What are you plotting now?' said Sooz, worriedly.

Dirk shrugged. He stood up, and walked to the door. 'There's a reason I asked you to meet me here, and it wasn't just so we could talk in secret.'

Sooz's eyes narrowed. 'What are you up to, you scheming tyrant?' she said.

'Scheming tyrant? Thanks, that's been one of my aspirational goals for a while now! Anyway, you leave me no choice, my little Moon Queen,' said Dirk.

'What do you mean?' said Sooz.

Suddenly Dirk darted out of the room and slammed the door shut.

'Hey!' screeched Sooz, her voice muffled from the inside of Hasdruban's office.

'Only I know the code to the door, Sooz. You're going nowhere!' said Dirk.

'What? You wouldn't dare!' said Sooz.

'I wouldn't dare? Hah, of course I would! You'll be OK, Sooz, there's food in the cupboard, and a bed in there. I'll come and get you after I've persuaded Chris to deal with Grousammer, I promise!'

'Come back here right now, you little monster!' shrieked Sooz from inside.

'Oh no, Sooz, sorry, but I can't have you running around ruining all my plans!' said Dirk.

'NOOooo… Let me out, let me out now!' said Sooz, hammering on the door.

Dirk marched into the room Chris had taken in the tower – a wide, windowed space near the top, airy and quiet. The White Wizard Christopher was sitting cross-legged, meditating. Rufino was next to him, also attempting to meditate, but not really succeeding.

'Greetings, your Dirkness,' said Rufino, getting to his feet.

'Grousammer sent me this,' said Dirk, holding a letter in his hand. 'It's for Christopher.'

Christopher opened his eyes and rose up serenely. A frown broke the tranquil stillness of his face.

'From the new Dark Lord? What does he want?' said Chris.

'Here, read it,' said Dirk, handing the letter to Chris. The letter, in scraggly, scratchy letters (Dirk's best attempt to forge Grousammer's handwriting), said:

Greetings, White One – or should I say
Christopher Purejoie? I know you, boy! And
I have your mother, Mrs Purejoie, locked up
in the Dungeon of Doom, along with your
absurd headmaster, Hasdruban!
Face me in battle – a great duel of the White
vs the Dark, and if you win, you can free
your mother. If I win, I shall feed all of you
to my vampires! Mwah, hah, hah!'

The White Wizard Christopher read the letter and sighed before passing it over to Rufino.

'What a waste of a mind, to be so obsessed with conquest and death. I feel sorry for Grousammer now that he has fallen so deeply into darkness,' said Christopher.

Dirk folded his arms. Sorry for him? That old bat, that usurping villain of villains, that beardless freak? Why would anyone feel sorry for him? Dirk shook his head. This holy stuff was weird.

Rufino frowned. 'Strange reading, this letter. Sounds more like…well, you, Dirk! It's like the sort of thing you would say.'

Dirk gulped. 'Umm…well…well he would, wouldn't he? Being a Dark Lord and everything – what would you expect?'

'I don't know, being this ex-headmaster thing you told me about, well, something a bit more… educated, I suppose,' said Rufino. 'Also, tactically it seems like a mistake. Why expose himself like this, when he is gaining the upper hand?'

'Educated? What do…? Actually, forget that. Whatever. Bad for him, good for us. You have to go and fight him, don't you, Christopher? One on one. I'll help you – together we can beat him!' said Dirk, doing a kind of shadow boxing, but instead of pretending he was in a fist fight, he acted as though he was in a great magical duel, casting mighty spells.

'Where is Sooz?' said Christopher, ignoring Dirk. 'I could do with her advice.'

'I haven't seen her,' said Rufino.

Dirk shrugged. 'Me neither,' he said. 'So, shall we ready an expedition? I can lead you a different way; we could bypass the army, find Grousammer and face him one on one!'

Chris shook his head. 'There will be no violence. I will go to him and surrender myself in exchange for my mother and Dr Hasdruban's freedom.'

'What? Are you mad?' shrieked Dirk.

'My Lord, that is not wise,' said Rufino. 'Surely it would be better to fight him, defeat this evil scourge once and for all!'

'No. I will not fight. There is only one path and that is the path of peace. It will be as I've said,' said Chris with a faint, saintly smile. With that, he began to walk.

'Hold on, where are you going?' said Dirk.

'To hand myself over to the enemy,' said Chris.

Dirk put his hands up to his head. 'No, no, no,' he muttered, 'this can't be happening!'

Fools Rush In...

Christopher walked slowly onward, his head held high, his hands clasped together in front of him, an expression of serene goodness on his face. He was on the road that led from the White Tower to the Darklands and he was going to give himself up in return for the freedom of his mother and his headmaster. He would martyr himself so that others might live. There could be no other way.

Rufino, Rosapina, Dirk and Bashar were waiting for him near the border. Slowly

Christopher drew near.

Rosapina stepped forward. 'With respect, your Holiness…'

Dirk made a face. They didn't call Christopher the White Wizard any more, they called him the Holy One or the Sainted One. They addressed him as 'your Holiness' and with much more respect than they afforded to Dirk.

Bah, sickening!

'With respect,' repeated Rosapina, 'we cannot allow you to go on and throw your life away like this!'

'It will be as it will be,' said Chris, barely slowing his pace.

'But don't you see, your loss would be a terrible blow to the people!' said Rufino.

'My loss? We would be gaining two other lives, just as worthy as mine. Is that worth the price?' said Chris beatifically.

Dirk shook his head in despair. This was beyond wishy-washy bleeding heart do-gooder nonsense – this was far worse! What had he created?

'Whatever, Chris,' said Dirk, running up to Chris's side. 'You can't just stroll in there like that. What's to stop him from locking you up with the rest of them? I mean, he's a Dark Lord – you can't trust him.'

Christopher the Sainted One replied, 'I will reason with him. Show him that honour and keeping your word are what define us, they make us what we are.'

'Oh, come on,' said Dirk, getting desperate now. 'Grousammer? He's not just any old Dark Lord, he's a Dark Lord that was once a teacher. You can't trust teachers, let alone Dark Lords! You know that!'

'We shall see,' said Christopher, walking onward.

Dirk shook his head in despair.

'It's no good, Dirk,' said Rosapina. 'We have to act.' She waved Rufino and Bashar forward.

'Seize him, carry him back to the tower, but do not harm him!'

'Yes, my lady,' said the Paladins.

'Sorry, sorry, sorry,' said Rufino as he marched up to Christopher, Bashar close behind, but Christopher simply ignored them.

'All is love,' he said softly and walked on. Rufino and Bashar tried to seize him. But as they drew near, their hands dropped to their sides. Peace fell across their faces. Love stayed their hands: it seemed like rough intent had turned to kindly compassion.

They looked back at Rosapina and shrugged. She moved in too, but nobody could touch Chris – all resolve seemed to fade to love at the last moment. His aura of gentle peace prevented any violence, no matter how well intentioned.

Dirk frowned. He wasn't so strongly affected. He could try to restrain Chris. But on the other hand, Dirk was a thirteen-year-old boy. Chris was a ten-foot tall angel. Dirk didn't have the strength, even if he could overcome the overwhelming urge to hug Christopher rather than to pin him down in an arm lock and carry him back to safety.

Christopher walked on. Dirk, Rosapina, Rufino and Bashar hung back.

'What shall we do?' said Bashar.

'We can't let him walk in there alone,' said Dirk.

'Indeed,' said Rosapina. 'But who will go with him?'

Rufino put his hand on Dirk's shoulder. 'We will go, won't we, Dirk?' he said.

Dirk looked up at him. Total madness! But… it was Christopher. And it was Dirk's fault.

'Of course, we have to, don't we?' Dirk said, and they set off after Christopher.

Rosapina and Bashar watched Chris, Rufino and Dirk continue down the road towards the Darklands.

'They're walking into almost certain death!

There's a horde of Goblins and Orcs in the way, not to mention an army of the undead,' said Bashar.

'Yet they will be walking with a living saint. Perhaps it will be enough,' said Rosapina.

Where Angels Do Not Fear to Tread

Christopher, Rufino and Dirk paced onward. They were drawing near to the borderlands, which gave on to the Plains of Desolation, where an army of Orcs, Goblins, ghouls, zombies and vampires waited for them…

'Where is my Lady Sooz?' said Rufino. 'I would have liked to have said goodbye to her.'

'Ummm…I don't know, but it's just as well, right? I'm glad Sooz isn't here. I miss her, sure, but this is almost certainly a suicide mission,' said Dirk.

'Indeed! You're right, it's better she's not here,' said Rufino.

'You do not have to accompany me,' said Chris. 'I would not hold it against you.'

'We're not leaving,' said Dirk. 'Aren't you worried that you're endangering us? By not turning back, you're forcing us to go with you, expose ourselves to danger.'

'Not at all. Love will prevail,' said Christopher.

Rufino and Dirk exchanged looks. Was he a saint? Or was he just mad? 'Almost certainly mad,' Dirk muttered to himself.

They were approaching a series of tall poles. On top cameras whirred and trained their lenses on them – CCTV cameras from earth. The enemy knew they were coming now. Sure enough, after a short while, an Orc patrol turned up, running down the road towards them – twenty Orcs in caps and chainmail blazers, with short-ruler swords.

'Grab 'em,' said the lead Orc. 'His nibs wants 'em alive!'

Rufino and Dirk pulled up short, Rufino reaching for his sword. But Christopher just walked on, forcing Dirk and Rufino to keep up with him.

The Orcs raced in, screaming and roaring, grinning ferociously. But as they drew near, their grins faded, their faces fell. They blinked up at Christopher as he smiled down at them. Swords were dropped from hands. Faces lit up with happy smiles – well, as far as an Orc's smile could be described as happy. 'Not angry' might be a better description. Some of them simply sat down. Others bowed their heads as he passed.

'Wow,' said Dirk, 'maybe this is going to work after all!'

'Hard to credit, isn't it?' said Rufino. 'He is indeed the Sainted One. He soothes the savage beast with peace and love.'

The three walked on. They began to draw near to the Plains of Desolation where the army was camped. Goblins and Orcs surrounded them, but every time they came within a certain distance of Christopher they paused. Their bloodcurdling shrieks and shouted threats turned to silence. Not a single Orc or Goblin tried to harm them. It was almost as if their hearts had been filled with love and peace. They stood, heads bowed, or they kneeled respectfully. Some of the bigger, tougher Orcs tried their best to put in a boot or two, but they could not.

'All is love,' said Christopher as he walked on.

Rufino and Dirk followed in his wake, amazed.

Soon they came to the black pavilions. Ghouls, tall, thin and skeletal, with skin stretched tight over bony skulls and teeth like needles, waited for them, along with battalions of zombies. But the ghouls and zombies could not endure Christopher's holy aura.

They simply fled, wailing.

The vampire lords remained inside their black velvet pavilions, unable to endure sunlight, let alone Chris's aura. Presumably they would wait for night to try their mettle.

They walked on, right up to the training fields outside the Gates of Doom, the entrance to the Iron Tower of Despair. And there was Grousammer, the Headmaster of Doom, waiting for them, standing in his black robes and hat, swishing his cane. He was flanked by Skabber Stormfart on one side and Lady Grieve, the Black Hag, on the other. Behind him were Orcs, Goblins, zombies and ghouls.

The Black Hag stepped forward. 'No further, not another step,' she hissed, her iron-taloned fingernails dripping with venom.

Skabber and Rufino, though, nodded at each other. Once they'd been allies of a sort.

Christopher came to a halt.

'What have we here?' said Grousammer. 'Dirk Lloyd, the naughtiest boy in school, Rufino, a disgraced prefect and a Paladin of questionable worth and…well, Christopher Purejoie, isn't it? You've changed, boy, haven't you?'

'I have come to offer myself up to you in return for my mother and Dr Hasdruban,' said Christopher without preamble.

'Your mother? What are you talking about?' said Grousammer.

Dirk gulped. This could be tricky!

'You kidnapped her, and sent me this ransom note,' said Chris, holding up the letter.

'Oh, please, what are you talking about, boy? I don't kidnap the parents of pupils! Who's going to pay their fees?'

'But then…who…' said Christopher in confusion.

Rufino narrowed his eyes in suspicion, and glanced over at Dirk. 'Did you…' he mouthed.

'No, no, of course not!' said Dirk.

Rufino folded his arms. 'If I find out that you—'

But the rest of his sentence was cut off by Chris. 'Well, it seems someone has deceived me,' he said, flicking a glance over at Dirk, 'but I shall deal with that later. In the meantime, there is still one you hold against his will. I offer myself up to you in return for the release of Hasdruban, then,' said Christopher, his voice loud and bell-like so all could hear.

Grousammer looked at Dirk, and then back at Chris. 'I'm not interested in you, Christopher Purejoie! What would I do with some kind of sainted fool like you? Sure, you should be punished for walking on the quadrangle grass without permission,' he said, pointing to the training grounds, 'but really it's hardly worth the bother. You're nothing to me!'

Chris blinked in surprise.

'Now that boy, there,' said Grousammer, pointing at Dirk with his cane. 'He's a bad boy, oh yes,' he went on, ruefully rubbing at his red, raw chin. 'I want him, indeed I do.

Hand him over to be dealt with properly and then I'll give you Hasdruban!'

Dirk looked back at Grousammer defiantly, and grinned his evil grin. Grousammer, Dark Lord though he was, actually flinched, which pleased Dirk greatly.

'Hand him over now!' said the Headmaster of Doom.

'I cannot command him, but if he wishes to give himself up, I will not stand in his way,' said Christopher.

'What? Don't be ridiculous,' said Dirk. 'I'm not giving myself up!'

'Why do you want him anyway? He's just a boy,' said Rufino.

'Hah, he's more than the naughtiest boy ever, we both know that. With him under my power I will reign supreme and then I can unleash my army of zomboys and schoolghouls…'

'Zombies,' said Dirk, 'it's pronounced zombies.'

Grousammer barely seemed to notice as he ranted. 'And they will overrun your wretched Commonwealth and feed on your brains!' said Grousammer. Then he sniggered, a sinister kind of 'tee, hee, hee' – Grousammer's version of a Mwah, hah, hah, perhaps.

He went on, a proper Dark Lord monologue. 'Don't you see? I'm the first Dark Lord ever to forge an alliance with the Clans of the Undead. I will rule this world for ever! All these zomboys are mine!'

'Yeah, whatever,' said Dirk, 'but it's zombies, not zomboys.'

'Silence, boy!' said Grousammer, who then took a step forward and aimed a blow at Dirk with his cane. He slashed him painfully across the legs. Grousammer certainly wasn't affected by Chris's aura of peace and love, that's for sure, thought Dirk as he grimaced in pain.

'Leave my friend alone!' said Christopher, sounding much more like the boy Christopher for the first time since he'd drunk of the essence. Finally, something was making him angry, thought Dirk to himself. He even felt kind of flattered that it was a threat to him personally that had set Chris off.

'I will not!' replied the Headmaster of Doom, stepping up to the Holy One and thrusting his chin into his face. 'That boy is mine and I'm going to give him 666 of the best, and when he's dead I'll bring him back as a zomboy slave to serve me for all time!'

'No you won't, not ever!' said Chris, angrily, and he raised his hands. Out burst a stream of silver energy, engulfing the Dark Lord Grousammer, who shrieked in pain. But then he pushed back, cutting at the clouds of glittering energy with his cane and dispersing them. His cane crackled with ebon power, gleaming like polished coal. He thwacked it down at Christopher but Chris pushed back, magical silver energy holding the cane in place.

They struggled like that, pushing back and forth, silver sparks and streaks of black magic spraying everywhere. Everyone around cowered back, unable to look at the sparks or to endure the black bolts.

'Finally,' said Dirk, 'it's actually working, a duel of wizards!'

'This was your plan all along, wasn't it, Dirk?' said Rufino, shielding his face from the titanic struggle between the Holy One and the Headmaster of Doom.

'Yes! Yes, it was! Isn't it an exciting duel? The Light versus the Dark, Good versus Evil, battling for ever across the aeons! How magnificent!' said Dirk. His face, bathed in a silver glow, looked quite mad.

'And what if Christopher loses? What if he is slain?' said Rufino angrily. 'You should not play with people's lives so!'

'Oh no, don't worry, Rufino, I'm an evil genius, sure, just not so much of the evil any more. I've got this covered,' said Dirk and he reached into his pocket and drew out an Anathema Crystal.

'Ah, I see!' said Rufino with a grin.

'Yup, I'll soon have them back to normal and everything will be all right!' said Dirk, putting a hand up to shield himself from the maelstrom, and trying to sneak his way closer to the duelling wizards.

Suddenly Dirk darted in and threw the crystal on to the ground, right in between Grousammer and Christopher, where it exploded in a flash of light. Dirk grinned his evil grin, readied his hands in front of him to give up a big 'Mwah, hah, hah' when…

Nothing happened.

Chris and Grousammer continued to struggle against each other, neither gaining the upper hand.

'You foolish boy,' shrieked Grousammer out of the corner of his mouth. 'I set up counters to those tawdry baubles months ago! I've studied your history, read your diaries, your records in the Dark Library. I know everything about you, boy! You can't outwit me – I am your headmaster!'

Dirk blinked up at him in surprise. He hadn't been expecting that! But then Dirk narrowed his eyes. He had one more trick up his sleeve.

Grousammer hacked at Chris with his cane. Christopher exuded a silvery cloud that absorbed the force of the cane like a pillow of energy. He pushed back, white lightning bursting from his fingertips, but Grousammer put his head down and his mortarboard hat expanded into a big black shield that absorbed the holy lightning. They struggled on.

Rufino, Skabber, the Black Hag and the zombies and ghouls stood there, open-mouthed in awed astonishment at the great battle.

Dirk wasn't finished yet, though. He muttered the words of a spell under his breath – and his left arm came away just above the elbow. He was using the spell of the Sinister Hand, one that he had used many times before. It allowed him to send off his arm on its own, to do stuff. Dirk grimaced in pain, as his arm squirmed for a moment on its own. It needed direction! He started to concentrate, guiding his separated arm with soul power[4].

His arm reached into Dirk's pocket – and pulled out a false beard! Dirk's arm scuttled over towards Grousammer. It tapped the Headmaster of Doom on the leg. Grousammer looked down… There was the disembodied arm, holding up his beard, his big red beard, the very one he used to wear back on earth before…

'Aiiiiiiiieeeeeeee!' screamed a terrified Grousammer.

You see, when Dirk first came to earth, he used the Sinister Hand spell to sneak his hand into Grousammer's room and shave off his beard! Grousammer had had nightmares about

---

[4] *See books one and two (*Dark Lord: The Teenage Years, *and* Dark Lord: A Fiend in Need *for plenty of examples of the Sinister Hand!*

it ever since. In fact, every day since, he shaved his chin two or three times just so he would never have a beard that could be shaved off by a disembodied hand again. That was why his chin was so red and raw...

'The horror,' howled Grousammer, 'the horror, the horror!' He wailed as he cowered back.

Christopher took advantage of Grousammer's sudden terror, silver energy bursting from his hands, and closed in on the Headmaster of Doom. The Dark Headmaster fell to his knees, still staring in horror at the beard.

'Now, help me now!' screamed Grousammer at the top of his voice.

And down from the skies swooped Gargon, seven feet tall, winged, taloned, scaled and massively strong. He plucked up Dirk and his sinister arm – beard and all – and flew away with him!

Rufino gazed up in astonishment. The Black

Hag cackled as Grousammer rose to his feet once more.

Christopher frowned. 'What have you done?' he said through gritted teeth.

'Hah, hah, the boy is mine!' sniggered the Headmaster of Doom.

'Return him to me!' said Chris, redoubling his efforts, forcing Grousammer back for a moment. And then Grousammer smiled.

'Sunset!' was all he said.

The sun began to sink behind the hills. Darkness spread across the land like a pool of blood and out of the darkness came the vampires – great vampire lords dressed in silken robes and velvet cloaks, bejewelled and armoured. The Lords of Sunless Keep, the great citadel of the dead. Soon Christopher and Rufino were surrounded by an army of the dead, though Christopher's aura kept them at bay. The vampires stalked and crept, glared and hissed, they beseeched and pleaded, threatened and cajoled – anything to get Chris to close down his aura or Rufino to come near enough for them to seize him and drink his blood.

But they could not lure him out or get closer than a few yards. For now… How long could Chris keep them at bay, especially whilst fighting a duel with the Dark Lord? Christopher was visibly tiring.

Grousammer said, 'This is going nowhere – time for you and me to have a chat, boy! Truce?'

Christopher paused. 'Truce,' he said.

'I have what I want – the boy Dirk. You are surrounded. But I will give you this, if you leave now,' said Grousammer, gesturing behind him with his cane. The Black Hag and Skabber dragged a figure out of the crowd and threw him down at Chris's feet.

Hasdruban! The old man rose unsteadily to his feet, adjusting his shattered glasses, smoothing down his once pure white robes

– now splattered with blood and grime – and smoothing out his long white beard.

'I'm so sorry, my dear boy,' he said, 'but they were just too strong for me!'

'Take him and leave. It's the best you can get from a bad situation,' said the Headmaster of Doom.

Christopher and Rufino exchanged looks.

Rufino whispered, 'Take it, your Holiness. Night has fallen, we are exposed! We'll come back for Dirk later.'

Christopher looked over at Grousammer and nodded. 'Agreed,' he said.

'Wise choice, my boy. Now get off the grass!' said Grousammer, pointing back the way they'd come with his cane before turning away and sniggering a 'tee, hee, hee'. The Black Hag turned away too, cackling. Skabber, though, he saluted Rufino whilst no one was looking.

Rufino acknowledged him with a nod.

Christopher meanwhile put an arm around

Hasdruban. 'It's all right, we're going to take you home now.'

'Really, back home? Oh, how lovely,' said Hasdruban. 'I've been so looking forward to a nice cup of camomile tea!'

Together, the three of them set off back to the White Tower, ghouls, zombies and vampires following along behind hissing and snarling, trying to get closer, but held at bay by Chris's holy aura – just. Slowly, ever so slowly, as Chris got more and more tired, his aura was shrinking and the dead were closing in.

Ghouls drew near, no more than a yard or two away, almost within reach. They snarled and growled, baring their teeth, raging at Rufino and Chris. Pale, wan and terrified, they continued on. Some vampire lords batted aside the ghouls, who whimpered and skulked back into the night. They closed in as near as they could get. The lords were so close that Chris and Rufino could smell them – they smelt of tomb incense and graves.

'Soon you will be ours and then we will feed!' said one.

'No, we'll draw it out, have a banquet, slowly drain them over days!' said another.

'Their blood will feed our children!' hissed one.

'Perhaps we'll bring Christopher back as a ghoul!' said a tall vampire queen.

'Rufino! Do you remember me?' said another.

Rufino looked over at him in surprise. 'Stefan of the Isles!' said Rufino.

'Yes, Rufino, it is I! I too was a Paladin once, but look at me now!' he said, preening, as he stood there in armour of burnished black, wearing a feathered helm and a red velvet robe. 'I am immortal! Join us, and you too could be immortal.'

Rufino shook his head. 'Your body is immortal but your soul burns in hell! I will never join you.'

'Hah, what makes you think you'll have a

choice?' screeched Stefan. 'They call me Stefan of the Viles now, and you too shall be renamed!' He leapt forward with fangs bared. But as soon as he connected with Christopher's aura Stefan's skin began to smoke and burn, and he had to lurch back into the darkness, howling.

After a few more nightmare hours and just when it seemed Chris would drop with fatigue and they'd fall to the ravening horde, they finally reached the Borderlands and the well-lit watch towers of the Commonwealth, manned by elvish archers whose eyes could see in the dark and whose arrows were deadly, enchanted to slay the dead once and for all. The vampires and their ghoulish minions weren't ready to assault the Commonwealth directly, and they knew it.

Not yet, anyway!

'Farewell, old friend, I'm sure we'll meet again,' called Stefan of the Viles from out of the darkness as the undead horde turned back to the night.

Carried Away

Dirk had been guiding the Sinister Hand, laughing to himself as he terrified the life out of Grousammer with his fake beard. What a genius I am, he thought.

Suddenly, all the air was knocked out of him and he was heading up into the sky! A scaled arm and taloned hand held him close. It was ferociously strong; Dirk could hardly move. He looked up…

'Gargon! What are you doing? Surely… not you… A traitor?' said an astonished Dirk.

Gargon was a seven-foot tall, winged, taloned and scaled…well, thing. But he wasn't so bad once you got to know him. And he was supposed to be Dirk's chief lieutenant.

'Sorry, Master – but Headmaster has my Lady!' said Gargon as he began to swoop down to the entrance to the tower – the Gates of Doom.

'Grousammer has Sooz? How?' said Dirk.

'He tortured code to Inner Sanctum out of Hasdruban – sent winged vampire lords in bat form to steal her from White Tower!' grunted Gargon as he landed.

'What? How did he know she was there?' said Dirk.

Gargon gripped Dirk as tightly as he could as he strode down the stairs of the tower to the lower levels. He also handed Dirk his disembodied arm, which Dirk proceeded to reattach. It began to seal itself back in place, leaving a nasty-looking lurid scar.

'Hasdruban have magical shell that can hear

everything in his sanctum, no matter where shell is. Headmaster of Doom confiscate it, Headmaster hear everything,' said Gargon in a voice like gravel in a blender.

Dirk slapped his head to his forehead. 'No, no! How could I have been so stupid?'

Gargon descended into the darkness below the tower. 'You could not know, why blame yourself?'

'I should have anticipated something like this. Anyway, where are you taking me?' said Dirk.

'Gargon going to throw you into Black Pit of a Thousand Lines.'

'What? The pit of what? Why?' said Dirk.

'Orders from Headmaster who release me from pit and say Gargon must do as he says or he will give Sooz 666 of the best. Moon Queen not survive that.'

'What about me? Will I survive being thrown into this pit?' said Dirk nervously.

'Oh, you survive in pit, sure. Me and Agrash, we survive. Whether Headmaster let you live after – that another matter!'

'What – you'd give me up to be killed?' said Dirk, aghast. 'You, my loyal lieutenant, Keeper of the Tower, captain of my Legions of Dread!'

'I am sorry, your Imperial Dirkness, I really am. Normally Gargon would be loyal, Master. But it simple. I love Lady Sooz, she is like little sister to me. You come second. And that that! What can I say?'

Dirk blinked up at him. Well, you can't argue with that, can you? he thought to himself as Gargon tossed him unceremoniously down into the depths of the Black Pit of a Thousand Lines as if he were nothing more than a discarded old boot.

Dirk landed in a pile of old stinking clothes – Orc and Goblin stuff, by the smell of them. Yuk! He got to his feet. Nearby was a little desk. And on the desk was a sheaf of papers. The top sheet read:

*Your punishment for being continuously naughty ever since
you came to school:*

1: Imprisonment in the Black Pit of a Thousand Lines

2: Writing out 1,000 times:
*'I recognise that Grousammer is the true Dark
Lord and not me, and I am deeply sorry for all my
past misdemeanours, especially for shaving off the
headmaster's beard.'*

Dirk shook his head. 'Grousammer is actually mad!' he said out loud but there was no one there to hear him.

He was alone, completely alone. At least it was dark, though that was a small comfort. But whatever way you looked at it, he'd been defeated and betrayed – outwitted by his enemy and stabbed in the back by his most loyal friend.

Dirk's shoulders slumped and his chin fell forward on to his chest.

All was lost.

Mother Knows Best

Dirk woke with a start.

'Hello down there?' squeaked a voice from above.

Dirk wiped the sleep from his eyes and looked up. 'Who's there?' he said.

'It's me, Agrash, your Imperial Dirkness!'

'Agrash! Good to hear your squeaky little Goblin voice. Have you come to get me out of here?' shouted Dirk from below.

'I'm afraid not, your Supremeness – I've only just got out of there myself!'

'What's up, then?' Dirk could see something hurtling down towards him, something small.

He stepped back. A small globule of snot landed just where he'd been standing. Dirk grimaced in disgust. Agrash was one of the most intelligent Goblins out there, which is why Dirk had promoted him, but he had a serious drawback – his long, warty nose continuously dripped snot.

'You've got a visitor, your Dark Majesty! Just getting ready to lower her down,' said Agrash.

'A visitor? What do you mean?' said Dirk.

'Right, she's on her way!' said Agrash. 'Ummm…good luck, sir!'

Dirk frowned up as an open cage was lowered down towards him. Inside was a tall, pale woman, her handsome features crisp and even, her skin like ivory, with black eyes, and ruby-red lips. Long black hair hung down to her waist – lustrous, shining, beautiful. She wore a bat-winged cloak, a velvet corset, a long skirt of deepest red and black leather boots.

Tiny fangs protruded over her ruby-red lips.

A vampire, and a queen too, judging by the pale silver tiara she wore on her head, thought Dirk.

Wait a minute…she looked like… No, it couldn't be!

'Hello, Dirkikins,' said the vampire in a rich, low voice – she sounded amused, sophisticated, confident.

Dirk's jaw dropped. 'Who… What's your name?'

'Don't you know, dear? Don't you recognise me?'

'WHAT'S YOUR NAME?' shouted Dirk.

'Why, it's Oksana, of course,' she said with a smile, revealing teeth that gleamed whiter than white, and were sharp as a shark's.

'Mother? How…after all this time… It's been thousands of years… How is this possible?'

'Oh, I conquered death a long time ago, you

know that, dear!' said Oksana – the vampire queen, and Dirk's real mother.

'But…but I saw you die! I saw Father plunge the stake in your heart. I saw him slaughter all the vampires – my cousins, my uncles, all of them!'

'Bah, that old fool! What did he know?' said Oksana.

'Wait, are you saying you weren't destroyed? How can that be?' said Dirk.

Oksana paused, putting a silk-gloved hand up to her chin. 'Well…umm…technically yes, I was…err…destroyed,' she said, waving the hand away. Dirk noticed many ruby-encrusted rings of gold on her fingers. 'Actually, it was this new Dark Lord. He found my old bones, brought me back to life with a terrible spell.'

'What, this absurd Headmaster of Doom? Grousammer? I struggled for millennia to find a spell that could do that. Nothing worked! How did he…?'

'Never mind all that, my little darling. Never

mind!' said Oksana, stepping forward and cradling Dirk's face in her hands. 'Let's just savour this reunion! We're back together again after all these years, my sweet little Dark Lordling.'

Dirk gazed up into her eyes. Could it really be the Dread Queen of the Night, the Dark Mistress of the Underworld, his mother, Oksana the Pale? Her eyes were like pools of liquid velvet, black as black could be, offering him the comforting warmth of the shadows, where he could be unseen, unheard, bathed in deep, dark silence, safe in his mother's dark love.

Tears welled up in Dirk's eyes. It had been so long, so long!

'Mummy,' he whispered as he gave himself up to her warm, dark embrace.

'So, my sweet little Dark Lordling,' she said, 'here's the deal.'

'Yes, Mother,' said Dirk, 'I'm listening.'

'If you accept him as your ruler, Grousammer will give you a post in his new regime!' she said.

'But, Mum…he took my throne! He stole everything from me,' said Dirk, 'I can't serve him, he's a…he's a teacher!'

'Now, now, Dirk, you know perfectly well you're not really bad enough to be the Evil One any more, don't you? Someone has to do it, and that someone has to be this Dark Headmaster.'

'Grousammer? Really?'

'Yes, dear – Grousammer. Trust me, Mummy knows best.'

'But why, why does he want me?' said Dirk.

'Well, he needs your experience, your knowledge. He'll make you his new Head Boy and together you can conquer the Darklands. With your evil genius and his power, you'll be unstoppable, and finally, after all these years, you and he will rule over everybody! It's what you always wanted, isn't it, my dark darling?'

Dirk blinked. It was true, it was what he'd wanted for thousands of years. Though he'd have preferred it if it was just him. Still…at least he'd be with his mum.

'And then, after that, well…' continued Oksana.

'After that, what?' said Dirk.

'Well, then…then it's earth…' she said silkily.

'What do you mean, earth?' said Dirk, warily.

'The headmaster and you will lead the Clans of the Undead to invade earth!' she said. 'With the human technology that Grousammer can teach us, a horde of Darkland Orcs and a vast army of the undead – well, we'd conquer earth, just like you dreamed of when you first arrived there!'

'But…but…vampires? And zombies? In Sussex? That'd be awful!' said Dirk.

'Mummy has to eat, dear, hasn't she?'

'But…but…' stammered Dirk.

'You wouldn't want Mummy to starve, now, would you…?'

'Oh, no…no, of course not. It's just…earth… all those people!' said Dirk, confused.

'I know! Yummity yum,' said his mother.

Dirk shook his head. 'I…I'm just not sure.'

'Now come on, dear, you don't want us to fall out now, after all these years.'

'Well… I guess. If you say so, Mummy,' said Dirk.

'Excellent, that's settled then. We'll have you out of this nasty little pit in a jiffy, and you'll be the new Head Boy with a nice new hat and everything.'

Dirk grimaced at the thought of it. Still, it had to be better than this pit!

Tea with Mummy

Dirk was sitting on a couch by a table laid out for tea in his mother's rooms in the Iron Tower. She'd summoned him for a 'chat'. He could guess what it was about. Dirk was supposed to swear allegiance to the headmaster and then he'd be made Head Boy, but he was dragging his feet. If he accepted the job, he'd be admitting that Grousammer was the real Dark Lord and Dirk was just his minion. He couldn't bring himself to do that.

Dirk stared at the floor. How could his mum

want him to be Head Boy? He was the rightful Dark Lord, he should be fighting back against Grousammer, with her supporting him. Why wasn't she on his side? His thoughts were interrupted by a small scraping sound. He looked up.

And there was his mother, Oksana the Pale, sitting in front of him. She stared at Dirk like a boa staring at a puppy. Dirk gazed back, wide-eyed. He still couldn't quite believe it. His mother, still alive after all these years? And why was she staring at him like that? That was the look she usually reserved for…well, dinner. Not him, her favourite 'little darkling'.

Almost as if she'd read his thoughts, Oksana smiled at him (revealing vampire fangs) and leant forward to pick up a black, red-trimmed tea pot.

'How would you like your tea, dear?' she said.

'Can't you remember, Mum?' said Dirk.

A flicker of irritation passed across her face.

'Don't ask silly questions, my little darkling,' she said.

'Well, it has been a while, I suppose,' said Dirk. 'I'll have it as I always do – black and bitter, like my heart!'

'Oh, very good dear, how lovely for you!'

She poured the tea into his mug – a white mug, of all things…except that around the rim, little dribbles of red had been painted on, so it looked like it was overflowing with blood. Dirk frowned. This tea business… Trouble was, he couldn't remember having tea before he fell to earth. He wasn't sure that it even existed in the Darklands before all this. No wonder his mother couldn't remember how he took his tea because there was no such thing back in the day. And where did she get this tea from, for a start?

'Anyway,' said Oksana, stepping over to sit next to Dirk. 'I wanted to have a little chat, my darkling boy.'

She put an arm around his shoulders. He

nestled in, slightly uncomfortably. It wasn't like a hug from Mrs Purejoie, thank evilness, and it was his real mum, but still. Hugs… Not really for him. He looked up at her pale, ruby-lipped face, framed by long lustrous black hair that shone in the moonlight from the tower windows. Actually, it felt pretty good, he had to admit – a dark embrace, somewhere to hide in the shadowed peace of her arms.

'I'm sorry, Mum,' said Dirk. 'I know you asked me to, but I just can't work for Grousammer, it's…'

Oksana interrupted him, hugged him closer, and whispered in his ear. 'Shhh, dear, shhh… Look, I found this…'

Dirk glanced down and he saw in her hand what looked like a human arm bone.

'My baby rattle!' said Dirk in astonishment. 'Where did you find it?' he added as he snatched it from her.

'The Night Nursery, back in Sunless Keep,'

said Oksana, 'in an old toy cupboard.'

The rattle was an ancient piece of yellowed bone with some black feathers hanging off one end and a silver chain ending in tiny little bells on the other. It looked like a fairly nondescript knick-knack (albeit made of bone) but to Dirk it was rich with memory.

'I used to pretend it was my staff of spells,' said Dirk, 'and wave it at…that nurse we had for a while, what was she called?' Dirk looked up at his mother, his eyes filling with tears from that long-forgotten time of sheltering darkness.

'Ummm…' said his mother, seemingly perplexed by the question.

'The Blood Nurse, that was it,' said Dirk, smiling at the memory. It hurt his brain a bit to recall it – after all, it was thousands of years ago, not to mention he could only have been about one or two. But he was a Dark Lord. His memory was not like an ordinary human's and the rattle had triggered a rush of forgotten images. He remembered his cot, also made from bone that had been varnished black. He remembered the mobile that had hung over it – little enchanted severed heads on silver chains that gave deep, sonorous chimes when they bumped together. They used to talk too, complaining about each other and exchanging insults. But mostly, they recited dark nursery rhymes like 'Four and Twenty Storm Crows Baked in a Pie', 'Bah, Bah, Black Creep,' 'Lumpty Grumpty Sat on a Wall', 'London Bridge is Falling Down, Because We Burned It to the Ground', or 'Sticks and Stones – We'll Break Their Bones', and other such fondly remembered rhymes.

Dirk smiled again, and held the old bone rattle to his breast.

'Now, my little Dark Lordling, about that Head Boy business…' cooed Oksana.

'Yes, Mummy, of course,' said Dirk compliantly, nestling further into her arms and burying his face in her moonlit hair.

Head Boy

Dirk stood on the right hand side of the Throne of Skulls, wearing a special hat that only prefects wore – a black boater, made of straw. It had Grousammer's seal on it – a grinning skull wearing a mortarboard with two crossed canes below and a motto in Latin – Timor liberabit vos (dread will make you free). He wore a black leather-armoured blazer (a battle blazer), a ridiculous pair of dark grey shorts and stupid schoolboy socks. He had a dark grey cape of office and a steel ruler sword at his side.

He was the Head Boy, chief amongst all the pupils of the School of Evil, as Grousammer had renamed his kingdom.

And he felt like a total idiot.

A bell rang, exactly like they did in schools back home on earth.

Dirk knew what that meant. He stepped forward and shouted into the PA system that Grousammer had installed in the tower.

'Attention, pupil minions, class time is over! Regiments...errrr, I mean forms 3a and 3b through to the upper fifth Goblin artillery class shall gather immediately in the Great Hall for assembly. Anyone late will get extra Black Tongue homework!'

His words echoed throughout the Iron Tower.

Goblins and Orcs began to file into the Great Hall of Gloom. Behind came the Headmaster of Doom, swishing his cane as he paced into the hall.

'You, Orc boy! Stop running in the corridor!'

he bellowed. 'And you, you horrible little Goblin! Stop that!'

The Orcs and Goblins began to form up in front of the throne. Previously, they'd been organised into companies and regiments, now they were organised into forms and houses. Dirk shook his head – the whole thing was insane! He'd much rather just leave all this behind and go and live with his mum in the Deadlands, in Sunless Keep where he had been born. But Grousammer still had Sooz locked up and he couldn't really abandon her. Could he? He sighed. No, he couldn't. And Mum was enjoying it too much here, anyway.

He sighed again – he'd been doing a lot of that recently.

Well, maybe they could turn the whole world into one big school. Sure, he wouldn't be the headmaster, but at least he'd be the Head Boy, and he could see his mum, the school Night Nurse, every day. Or every night. And if he did well and earned Grousammer's trust, maybe he could get Sooz released.

Grousammer paced up to the throne and sat down. It groaned in welcome. He turned to Dirk. 'I found this, boy. What are you going to do about it?' he said, handing Dirk a book.

The book was called *Skirrits: An Anthropological Study*.

'What about it, Headmaster?' said Dirk, confused.

'You checked it out of the Dark Library,' said the Headmaster of Doom.

'Yeah, so?' said Dirk.

'Five hundred years ago! It's seriously overdue, boy. Do you have any idea of the size of the fine?'

'I…umm…' sputtered Dirk, caught off guard.

'Oh, never mind,' said the Headmaster, snatching it back. 'You'll just have to do extra homework for me until you've paid it off!'

Dirk stared up at him. 'You can't be serious!' he said.

'Oh, you don't think I'm serious, do you?' Grousammer said. He gestured, waving someone forward. The Black Hag stepped up, dragging someone behind her – someone in chains.

'Sooz!' said Dirk. She was chained and gagged, so she couldn't run or speak. She stared at Dirk, trying to say something, but to no avail. Instead she just glared at him.

Why would she be angry with me? thought Dirk. Wait a minute… Oh yeah…

The Black Hag cackled, and traced an envenomed talon down Sooz's cheek.

Dirk's eyes widened in horror – one cut from that claw and Sooz would die in seconds! 'All right, all right, please, sir, I'm sorry, sir, I'll pay the fine, I'm sorry my library book was so overdue!' said Dirk desperately.

'OK, then, just a little reminder of who's holding the cane, here,' said the Headmaster, waving the Black Hag away. 'Take her back to the Borstal Wing, and let's get on with the assembly.'

The Borstal Wing. That was what Grousammer called the old Dungeons of Doom. Ridiculous, thought Dirk.

The Headmaster of Doom stood up.

'Now, listen, Goblin boys and girls. I have an announcement. There is to be a new curriculum, and a whole new exam system!'

There was a collective groan from the assembled pupils.

'Quiet!' shrieked Grousammer, slapping his cane into his other hand.

Everyone went as silent as the grave, immediately – well, except that the graves weren't so silent around here any more... You could have heard a pin drop. Dirk had to admit, this part of Grousammer's new regime was impressive. Harsh discipline. It was better obedience than Dirk could ever achieve when he had been the Dark Lord.

Grousammer went on. 'There will be a new GCSE – or Goblin Certificate of Sinister Education. Subjects will include Elf Slaying, Castle Siege, Massacre Training, Earth Technology 101, Baking Hobbit Pie and Ruler Sharpening, to name but a few. For those most advanced pupils of the Six-Six-Sixth Form there will be Evil Levels – we'll call them E-Levels. After that, there will be a higher education degree system with grades such as First Degree Murder, Second Degree Murder and so on.'

The assembled Orcs and Goblins stared up at Grousammer, confusion and fear written all over their faces.

'Now, as to the appointment of prefects, monitors and sneaks – advancement will be based on the demerit system. You get extra demerits for bullying, informing on your fellow pupils and lying – to each other, but never to a teacher! Those with the most demerits can expect fast and rapid promotion. Clear?'

The Orcs and Goblins shuffled and muttered and looked…baffled.

'CLEAR?' bellowed Grousammer.

'Yes, sir, Headmaster, sir!' shouted the assembly in a cacophony of Goblin squeals and Orcish roars that made Dirk wince.

'Good. And remember the purpose of the new curriculum is to train you all to assimilate the Commonwealth into our school. And then… we'll invade a whole new world! Where you will all be prefects and monitors and the humans will be your year-one pipsqueak squirts to bully and give detentions to as much as you like. We will unleash the zomboy apocalypse on earth!'

'The zombIE apocalypse, zombIE,' muttered Dirk to himself.

The assembly of Orcs and Goblins continued to stare, nonplussed. What was he talking about? Zomboy apocalypse? Year-one pipsqueak squirts?

Dirk moved alongside and hissed at them,

'Cheer, you fools, cheer!'

The Black Hag, Skabber Stormfart, Gargon and Agrash were all doing the same – walking through the assembled ranks and encouraging them to cheer. No one wanted an angry headmaster!

Grousammer began to swish his cane with irritation. Finally the Orcs and Goblins got it and the hall erupted in a great cheer.

'Hurrah for the Headmaster of Doom! Hurrah!' they howled, each one of them terrified of getting six of the best. Or worse – such as a thousand lines when you didn't even know how to write in the first place.

Later, once the assembly had been dismissed and Dirk was left with a little free time, he made his way over to another new innovation that had been set up in the tower – the ruck shop. It sold sweets for the pupils of the School of Evil.

Dirk, curious, examined the wares. Laid out

were various 'delicacies' – Black Sherbet, Acid Drops (made with actual acid), Trouble-Gum, Iron Bars, Chocolate by Death, Goodstoppers, Helly Babies, Whine Gums, and so on.

Dirk shook his head. A sweet shop in the Iron Tower of Despair? Everything he'd ever created had been turned into some kind of school-of-horrors freak show!

'Greetings, Master!' said a squeaky voice from the back of the shop. 'Do you want to buy something?'

'Agrash? What are you doing there?' said Dirk.

'Well,' said Agrash, 'the headmaster let me out of the pit after I did my lines...'

'What were you in for – sending Dave to me with that message?' said Dirk.

'Yes, your Awesomeness. But he seems to have forgiven me for now. Well, as long as I do as I'm told, like taking your mum to meet you.'

'So, this is your reward, working at this... what do you call it?'

'The ruck shop. The Dark Headmaster said I couldn't be trusted and I wasn't up to doing anything more than running a sweet shop. So I took him at his word. He actually approved!'

'Good for you, Agrash.'

As they talked, Dirk's mum approached the shop.

'Good evening, dear,' she said. 'Would you like me to buy you a sweetie?'

Dirk looked up at her. 'I'd love some Goodstoppers, Mum!' he said.

She smiled down at him. 'Of course, my dark little Lordling,' she said and she turned to order some from Agrash.

Dirk frowned up at her back. This was all very well, but he was getting a little uncomfortable about the way things were going with his mother. OK, he was trapped in the body of a thirteen-year-old boy, but he wasn't actually a thirteen-year-old boy, and she shouldn't really be talking to him as if he were. It had been nice at first, but now…well, it felt a bit cloying, like having two Mrs Purejoies, even if one was an Anglican Reverend and the other an ancient and powerful vampire queen and Dread Mistress of the Underworld.

Oksana bought a bag of Goodstoppers and handed them to Dirk.

'Here you are, my sweet little ball of hate,' she said cooingly.

By the Nine Hells, it was exactly the same feeling he had when Mrs Purejoie wanted to give him hugs, thought Dirk. Which was quite often, for some reason. Perhaps if Mrs Purejoie could see into his heart, she wouldn't have been so affectionate. Mind you, if his real mum could see into his black and bitter heart she'd probably give him extra hugs! Anyway, he'd better have a word with Oksana – it couldn't go on like this.

'Mum, listen. I'm not really a kid any more. This body is a curse that Hasdruban laid on me. You know, I used to be as tall as the headmaster,

I had big horns, and hooves and talons… It's still me, inside this body.'

'You'll always be a sweet little monster to me!' she said, tweaking his cheek.

'Hey! Still me inside – the Dark Lord. Thousands of years old. I built this tower, fought battles with vast armies, burnt cities, cast great spells that covered the sky in gloom. They called me the Evil One – I was feared by everyone, loved by none. I'm not your little kid any more, Mother.'

'Well, that was then, dear, but all that's gone, along with the essence. Now you're just a boy with… How shall I put it? A chequered past.'

'A chequered past! Hah, that's one way to put it, I guess. A past that goes all the way back to my dad murdering my mother, all those years ago!' said Dirk.

'Well…it was so long ago, let's not dwell on it,' she said.

'But I've been trying to get revenge ever since,

Mum, ever since!' said Dirk.

'Why, dear, is your father still alive?'

'Still alive? How could he possibly still be alive?' said Dirk.

'Well, vampires can live forever, can't they?' said Oksana, looking a little flustered.

'What? Dad wasn't a vampire!' said Dirk, astonished.

'Oh, ahh…' said Oksana. 'Umm…it's so long ago, remind me again…'

Dirk narrowed his eyes suspiciously. 'You know…you enchanted him, trapped him in Sunless Keep…'

'Oh yes, of course, I remember now,' said Oksana. 'Handsome fella…called… Oh, what was it now?'

Dirk folded his arms. 'Gamulus the Good.'

'Good? He was good? Really?' said Oksana.

'Yeah, he was the first White Wizard. You trapped him, married him. But then he escaped…'

'Of course, yes, of course, now I remember…
How silly of me!' said Oksana shiftily.

Dirk went on. 'And returned with an army of
Paladins, staked everyone to death and carried
me off and tried to bring me up as his do-gooding
patsy… I can't believe you've forgotten!'

'Well, it really was a long, long, time ago,'
said Oksana. 'Anyway, no time to chat,' she said,
'must get on. Enjoy your sweets, my dark little
Lordling.'

Oksana turned and walked away. Dirk
frowned. Something wasn't right, not right at
all. He put a hand to his chin. He'd been so
happy to be reunited with his mother, perhaps
he'd lost sight of the things he really believed in.
Dirk looked over at Agrash speculatively, and
stared in fascination as a globule of snot grew at
the end of his nose…and plopped, to land with
a splash on a tray of acid drops. Dirk blinked.

'Errr…here you are, Agrash,' he said,
handing him the bag of Goodstoppers. 'I don't

think I want them after all.'

'Oh! Oh, well, OK, then, your Dirkness,' said Agrash.

Dirk turned away, deep in thought. After a few minutes he said, 'Agrash?'

'Yes, Master?'

'It's time we got Sooz out of jail, don't you think?' said Dirk.

Delivered from Evil?

Dirk and Agrash walked down the stairs towards the dungeons beneath the tower. Dirk was dressed in his full Head Boy outfit; Agrash carried a big tray full of ruck shop sweets.

Where once a big sign had said:

THE DUNGEONS OF DOOM

it now read:

> ### THE BORSTAL WING
> For the retraining of the excluded, the
> suspended and the expelled

Dirk shook his head. What a mess Grousammer had made of his wonderful tower. The Borstal Wing? Pah! The Dungeons of Doom – what was wrong with that? No mucking about, everyone knew where they stood with the Dungeons of Doom. They were dungeons. Where you'd probably meet your Doom. Simple.

Anyway, whatever. The sooner they were out of here the better. Dirk would get Sooz out of jail, see her to safety and then see whether he could persuade his mum to come with him. If she really was his mum… He was beginning to have his doubts.

At the bottom of the long, dark stairwell, they came to a dimly lit foyer where two Orc prefects guarded the entrance to the cells and torture chambers beyond, their caps askew on their heads, and their shorts stained with food and grime.

'Greetings,' said Dirk. 'The headmaster wants to see the schoolghoul called Susan Black – the so-called Moon Queen.'

'Yeah?' said one of the Orcs. 'Have you got one of 'em report cards wiv his signature on?'

'I'm the Head Boy, I don't need a pass,' said Dirk with all the authority he could muster.

The Orcs blinked at him. He was the Head Boy. And he used to be the Dark Lord. And he sounded like he knew what he was doing. They looked at each other.

Agrash stepped forward with the tray covered in sweets. ''Ere you go, boys,' he squeaked, 'have a break!'

'Cor, fantastic,' said one of the Orcs.

'Helly Babies! I love 'em,' said the other, and they both started stuffing their faces, chomping and chewing, making horrible slurpy sounds as they did so. Orcs. What could you expect?

'Keys,' said Dirk, 'where are they?'

'Wha…?' said one of the Orcs, his mouth full of Goodstoppers. 'Oh, yeth, over there, onna wall…'

Agrash kept the Orcs fed, whilst Dirk picked up the keys and walked into the Borstal Wing. It was lit poorly by torches on the wall, and it was dark and dirty. Cells lined the corridor. Most were empty these days, as Grousammer preferred to use the Black Pit and some short, sharp strokes of the cane as punishment, but once the Dungeons of Doom had been bustling with prisoners.

Ah, the good old days, thought Dirk to himself.

Dirk found Sooz's cell fairly easily. He unlocked it and strode in. Sooz was sitting in the corner, writing. She looked up in surprise – and immediately rose to her feet and pointed an accusing finger at Dirk.

'You lied to me, you lying liar!' she said.

'And your point is?' said Dirk.

'And you locked me up and let me get kidnapped by vampires. How could you?' said Sooz.

'Dark Lord,' was all Dirk said, shrugging a 'what do you expect?' shrug.

Sooz narrowed her eyes and bunched her fists.

'Ooooh…you…'

'At least I've come to rescue you, haven't I?' said Dirk.

'And what took you so long? I've been in here for days!' snapped Sooz.

'My mum…' said Dirk, frowning.

'What, Mrs Purejoie? Don't tell me she really was kidnapped!' said Sooz, her anger turning to shocked concern.

'No, no, my real mum. Maybe. If it's really her,' said Dirk, looking a tad forlorn, tears welling up in his eyes. And that was a rare thing indeed, Dirk getting all choked up.

Sooz's face changed from anger to compassion

in a moment. She couldn't help herself – she went up and put an arm around him.

'Tell me about your mum,' said Sooz. 'What's her name, for a start?'

'Oksana the Pale,' said Dirk.

'What's she like? Nice? Kind? Like most mums – you know, looks after you and puts a plaster on your cuts? Nothing like mumsy hugs to make you feel better, right?' said Sooz.

'Ah…umm… No, not really. And as for cuts… Not a plaster so much as… Well…it's really best not to get cut in front of her,' said Dirk.

'What's her second name?' said Sooz.

'It's more of a title really,' said Dirk, uncomfortably.

'Really? She's like an aristocrat or something?'

'Yes, you could say that. Her full title is…well, it's "Dread Mistress of the Underworld"…style of thing,' said Dirk.

'Oh!' said Sooz in surprised tones. Her arm dropped, as she put a hand to her mouth.

'Right… And what does she…well, do?' said Sooz.

'She's a vampire. A queen of the vampires in fact. Unfortunate, but there you go,' said Dirk.

'Oh, I see. Actually that makes…sense…' said Sooz, looking a little embarrassed. 'So, she's still alive, after…what, how many years?'

'Thousands,' said Dirk, 'but to be honest I'm not entirely sure if it really is her. It could be some kind of trick by the Headmaster of Doom to get me to do what he wants. Or maybe it is her and she's just getting a bit forgetful with old age. I mean, she really is old and she got brought back to life and stuff. That can cause memory loss, I'm sure.'

'If it's a trick, that's cruel. Very cruel,' said Sooz.

'Well, yes. But then Grousammer is a Dark Lord, after all. Anyway, we have to get going. What were you writing – a letter?' said Dirk, walking over to take a look. There was a sheaf of papers, covered in Sooz's handwriting.

SUSAN BLACK

Your punishment for your gross insubordination and rebellious attitude:

1: Rehabilitation in the Borstal Wing

2: Writing out 1,000 times:
'I will not wear make-up and jewellery in school assembly and I will never talk back to the Dark Headmaster again.'

'Hah, I see, the usual reasons, even when you were back home on earth. At least I've saved you from having to write that out a thousand times,' said Dirk.

'Yup, at least there's that. Now let's get out of here!'

A Dark Horse

Together they made their way up to the entrance. The two Orc prefects were fast asleep, their bellies distended and swollen, having stuffed their faces with every last sweet on the tray.

Agrash was there too, looking rather pleased that he had been able to take out two Orcs on his own. With sweets.

'Aggie!' said Sooz, rushing over to give the Goblin a hug.

'Mistress, it is good to see you. I can't wait to

get out of here and back to your earth, where I can rap in your band again!'

Dirk stared in amusement as they hugged. Agrash's nose stuck out over Sooz's shoulder and a little drop of snot fell down her back.

'Yeah, Aggy Z, back in da house!' said Sooz, leaning back and laughing.

Agrash thrashed his right hand down in a kind of 'gangsta' gesture, but he did it too vigorously, and this time it was a spray of snot that flew from the end of his nose.

Sooz leaped back in disgust.

'Sorry, my lady,' said Agrash, pulling a filthy handkerchief out of his pocket and wiping his long, green, warty nose.

'Well, what a charming reunion! Anyway, time to move on, folks – we've got to get out of here and meet up with Gargon,' said Dirk.

'Old Gargy too? Great!' said Sooz.

'Yeah, he's going to fly you out of here. Now, being an Evil Genius and all that, I chose today for the breakout because it's Bad Sports Day at the School of Evil. So most of the Orcs and Goblins will be playing stuff like Rugby Deathball, Foothead, Running for your Life, Wrathletics and stuff.'

'Bad Sports Day? Really?' said Sooz.

'Yeah, don't ask! Anyway, we should be able to walk out of here unnoticed. Then Gargon can fly you back to the White Tower where you'll be safe with Christopher.'

'Christopher! Is he still…?' said Sooz, accusingly.

'Yes, yes, he's still a freakin' saint,' said Dirk.

'You should never have done that to him!' said Sooz.

'All right, all right, but for now, can we just get you home? Is that OK?'

'What do mean, "get me home"? Aren't you coming?' said Sooz.

'No, I'm staying here with my mum,' said Dirk.

'Are you sure? Won't you get in trouble for breaking me out?'

'Maybe, if anyone finds out. Or maybe I can persuade Mum to leave too. I dunno,' said Dirk. 'I haven't really worked that bit out yet.'

They headed up the stairs to the main entrance of the Iron Tower, a large circular chamber with an ebon floor of shiny black marble that threw up a ghostly glow when anyone stood on it, to light their way. All around the chamber, doors led off to various places – kitchens, servants' quarters, barracks, administrative offices and so on. Two great staircases climbed up to the Great Hall of Gloom, or the Assembly Hall of Gloom as Grousammer had renamed it.

The great Gates of Doom that led out to the outside were open at the moment and bright sunlight spilled into the chamber. Beyond, on the Training Grounds, masses of Orcs and Goblins were milling around watching various sporting displays and games.

Out of the shadows stepped a hideous winged figure, smoke snorting from its nostrils, demon-faced, red-eyed and fanged.

'Gargy!' screamed Sooz.

A big smile split Gargon's monster face as Sooz ran over to greet him with a hug.

'My lady, so good to see you safe!' said Gargon, tenderly.

Dirk shook his head. OK, it was one thing to see Sooz being matey with a Goblin, but having a seven-foot tall demon as one of your BFFs? That was something else, he thought. Also, it annoyed him that Gargon was loyal to her and not to him any more. OK, he'd kind of forgiven Gargon for betraying him – Dirk would have done the same, after all – but still. It irked. Why Sooz over him?

Anyway, what could he do? Time to move on.

'OK then, let's get outside. As soon as we're in open space, Gargon can fly away with Sooz.'

Sooz's eyes widened with worry. 'All the way

to the White Tower?'

'Gargon not able to fly that long with my lady, but we just have to make it to the Scarp Hills at the edge of Plains. Shouldn't be too hard. Maybe we must rest along the way after that.'

'Well, doesn't that sound just dandy,' said a voice and into the chamber stepped Oksana, Dirk's mother. 'Planning to sneak off without telling your mother, eh? You naughty boy!'

'Mum, no, no!' said Dirk, his face full of guilty panic. 'I wasn't sneaking off, just—'

'Just breaking that juvenile delinquent out of jail without the headmaster's permission?' said Oksana, pointing at Sooz with a long-nailed finger and edging a little closer.

Sooz moved nearer to Gargon, who put a protective arm around her.

Dirk stepped behind Agrash without thinking.

'Hey!' said Agrash, hopping back behind Dirk.

Oksana smiled a fanged smile at their antics, clearly enjoying the fear in their eyes.

'Well, you've got me there, but... Look, Mum, we don't have to stay here! My friends can go back to the Commonwealth where they'll be safe – and you and me, we could go home! Go back to Sunless Keep where we could live away from all this. What do you say?'

'We can't do that, dear – after all, I owe the Headmaster of Doom. He did bring me back with that...umm...that spell thingy,' said Oksana.

Dirk frowned. 'Wait a minute...' he said slowly. 'You just walked in here!'

'Eh? So?' said Oksana.

'It's blazing sunlight outside. You shouldn't be able to go out on a cloudy day, let alone in that!' said Dirk.

Oksana's face fell. 'Errr...the headmaster, he did another spell thing to let me walk in the sun!'

'No way!' said Dirk, stepping forward. 'You're not my mum, are you? It's all a lie!'

'No, no, dear, of course I am. You're my little Dark Lordling, really, you are, my little black-hearted sweetheart, you know it's true,' said Oksana. Now it was her turn to step back.

'Lies! You can't remember who my father is! You can't even remember how you died! And you're just strolling about in the sun like it's nothing. You're not even a vampire, are you?' shouted Dirk accusingly.

'Shut up, you naughty boy!' said an increasingly desperate-sounding Oksana. 'Go to your room, now, and then to bed without any supper!'

'Oh, don't be ridiculous, I'm not ten years old any more. I'm not even a hundred years old any more!' said Dirk.

Sooz, Gargon and Agrash were following the exchange in open-mouthed fascination, their heads moving back and forth as if they were at a tennis match.

'You're going to be in so much trouble...' said

Oksana, wagging her finger at Dirk.

'Shut up!' screamed Dirk so forcefully that Oksana had no choice but to fall silent.

Dirk went on. 'You're not my mother! You're not even a vampire. I can't believe I fell for this nonsense. I'm not having it any more, I'm not working for that old fraud Grousammer!'

Oksana put a hand to her mouth in shock. 'Don't say that!' she hissed.

'I'm not going to give up on the Throne of Skulls, it's mine, and I'm going to take it back from the usurper. Headmaster? Bah! He's nothing but a beardless loon!' said Dirk.

Sooz and Gargon and Agrash exchanged smiling glances. It looked like their old Dirk was back!

Suddenly Oksana snarled, 'You will fail! And be thrown into the pit, where you will rot until the headmaster decides to cane you to death with 666 of the best!'

And then she began to change… Her body

started to morph and shift like an animated clay figure. Everyone stared in surprise as her legs seemed to merge together to form a long green-scaled snake body with the torso and head of a woman. She had long brown hair and grey-green eyes, and two little horns on her forehead.

'Lucina the Lamia!' said Agrash.

'A shape changer! Hah, that explains it, you're not my mum – you never were!' said Dirk.

'Of course not, you stupid boy, I'm a Lamia, and I serve the real Dark Lord, not some pitiful earth kid who just thinks he's a Dark Lord!' said Lucina.

Gargon stepped forward and growled. Lucina went pale. Instantly she darted back and slithered as fast as she could out of the door.

'Stop her,' said Dirk, 'she'll warn the others!'

Gargon leaped forward, but it was too late. Lucina was already out of the main gate and shouting for help. Agrash, Sooz, Dirk and Gargon raced out after her, but she started changing shape once more – within a moment she was a cheetah, and racing away faster than any of them could possibly run.

It was just as well it was Bad Sports Day. All the 'school pupils' were watching the games and were making a lot of noise, cheering and shouting. Lucina hadn't got to them yet, but it was only a matter of time…

'There's no time to waste – take Sooz and fly, Gargon, fly!' said Dirk.

'Yes, Master!' he said.

'But what about you and Aggy?' said Sooz.

'Don't worry about us, I'll think of something,' said Dirk.

'By my nose, I hope so!' said Agrash.

'Go,' said Dirk to the other two. 'There's nothing you can do here anyway!'

Sooz nodded, turned to Gargon and put her arms up. He tenderly picked her up and flapped skyward.

'See you laterrrr…' said Sooz, her voice

fading away on the wind.

'I hope you can think of a good plan, your Slyness,' said Agrash, wiping his nose (it dripped even more when he was stressed). Peering towards the training grounds, Dirk and Agrash could see that Lucina had reached what looked like a little podium overlooking the Rugby Deathball field (ogre scrums, Orcish backs, Goblin wingers, captured human referee). Grousammer would be sitting there, no doubt.

'I knew that old fraud Grousammer wasn't good enough to find a spell that could have brought my real mother back to life. He couldn't have been better than me, never!'

'Come on, Sire, forget about all that, we need a cunning plan…now!' muttered Agrash, nibbling at the yellowing nail of his green Goblin thumb.

'What? Oh yes, of course.' Dirk grabbed Agrash by the shoulder. 'Follow me!' he yelled and they began to run round the tower, heading for the rear area. Dirk took a look over his shoulder. He could see Grousammer standing up, towering over the Orcs and Goblins around him. He was clearly shouting and pointing over at the tower. A force of Orcs began to head over in their direction…

'Faster!' said Dirk, and they dashed around the tower. Soon they were running into the shadows at the rear, out of the sun.

'Where…' Pant, pant… 'Are we…' Pant, pant… 'Going…?' gasped Agrash.

'Shut up and save your breath,' said Dirk, just as he turned into a wide-open doorway set into the base of the back of the tower.

'Ah,' said Agrash, 'the Dark Stables!'

'Yup,' said Dirk, dashing in. The stable was lined with several large stalls, some of them holding enormous black stallions. But they weren't ordinary stallions, oh no. They were NightMares, with yellow eyes, iron hooves, shiny black coats and breath that snorted from their nostrils in sulphurous clouds.

Dirk opened one of the stalls and out leaped a stallion with an echoing, hellish neigh. It pawed the ground with its hooves, setting off sparks from the cobbled yard.

Dirk put his hand up and stroked its muzzle.

'Blackheart, my beauty,' said Dirk, 'do you remember me?'

The horse snuffled in recognition. He would always know his master, no matter what form he took. It was Dirk who had created the NightMares, breeding them from ordinary horses, adding a touch of black magic and a hint of hell, so long ago that even he'd forgotten when.

'We must fly away from here, Blackheart,' said Dirk, and he swung himself up and on to the horse's back. The horse whinnied a spectral greeting, eager to be on the move.

'Agrash, let's go!' said Dirk, reaching down a hand and hauling up the little Goblin to sit behind him. They looked like two little dolls on the back of a great, black rocking horse.

'Run, Blackheart, run,' said Dirk into the NightMare's ear.

Blackheart rose up on his hind legs, gave a great whinny and galloped out of the stables at breakneck speed, hooves throwing up sparks at every step, nostrils snorting out smoky clouds of sulphur, yellow eyes blazing. Dirk had to wrap his hands into Blackheart's streaming mane, whilst Agrash had to fasten both his arms around Dirk to stay on.

They hurtled away out of the tower.

'To the Borderlands, Blackheart, to the Borderlands, and then on to the White Tower!' said Dirk. They burst out of the lee of the tower into bright sunlight…and almost into the arms of a company of Orcs! There was Skabber Stormfart, the Orc prefect, and at least twenty more behind him.

Blackheart veered away, but Skabber was

right there, big, hulking and strong. He darted in and reached up to Dirk, about to pluck him off Blackheart's back!

But Skabber missed his grab – deliberately, it seemed to Dirk – and fell to the ground, making it look as though he had tried and failed, rather than just letting Dirk get away, which Dirk thought must have been in his heart. The other Orcs seemed unconvinced but it didn't matter – Blackheart surged away, his hooves pounding the ground like hammers on an anvil. Soon they were racing away into the distance. Behind them they could hear the voice of Grousammer.

'NOOOOOOooooooooooooo!'

Dirk grinned, put his head back, and let out a happy 'Mwah, hah, hah!' And then he frowned. What was that dribbling down his back, making his shirt all sticky? No…not…it couldn't be – aargh, it was! Snot!

'Agrash, you filthy little Goblin!' said a disgusted Dirk.

'I'm sorry, Master, I'm sorry, all that excitement was just too much for me!'

Really? That's the Plan?

Dirk was sitting in his room in the White Tower, staring out the window. Agrash, Gargon, Sooz and Dirk had all made it safely back, Gargon flying Sooz home, and Dirk and Agrash travelling all the way on Blackheart's mighty back.

Blackheart had been stabled in the White Tower but the grooms had a bit of a hard time with him. He didn't really fit in with the rest of the horses (all the Paladins of the Whiteshields were mounted on white stallions, naturally), and in the end Dirk had to tell him to go home on his own. He'd be fine once he got back to the Dark Stables. That was where he belonged. And nobody was going to give him any trouble along the way. Wolves avoided NightMares. Actually, everything avoided NightMares if they could.

That had been the day before. This morning, Dirk had actually been summoned by Christopher, the Holy One, for a 'strategy meeting' with Sooz, Rufino and Rosapina.

Summoned by Christopher? It's usually me who does the summoning, he thought to himself. But still, here he was in the White Tower, and Chris was now the White Wizard. Or the Holy One, as the do-gooding dupes of the Commonwealth called him. It was Chris's domain, technically.

Dirk sighed. It was nearly time for the meeting, but right now he was staring out of the window. He was feeling rather sad. Next to him, Dave the Storm Crow, echoing his master's mood, also stared out of the window forlornly. A tear welled up in Dirk's eye just as there was a knock on the door.

'Come in,' said Dirk.

Sooz opened the door and walked in. Dirk looked up at her, his lower lip wobbling.

'Dirk! What's wrong?' said Sooz, stepping up to him and putting an arm around his shoulders. This was the second time in as many days that she'd seen Dirk almost cry. This was unheard of!

'It's Mum,' said Dirk.

'But she was fake, she wasn't your mum. It was a mean trick by nasty old Grousammer,' said Sooz.

'I know, but don't you see? It means my mum, my real mum, really is dead. Proper dead and buried. For a moment there I believed she'd come back, but it was all make believe.'

'Oh, I see. Poor Dirk,' said Sooz.

'It's like I'm having to mourn her all over again,' he muttered.

'Ah, there, there, Dirk,' said Sooz solicitously, and she kissed him on the top of his head.

'Hey, do you mind!' said Dirk, shrugging her arm off. 'It's not that bad!'

'All right, all right, keep your hair on,' said Sooz, folding her arms and looking rather peeved.

'Keep my hair…on?' said Dirk, patting the top of his head. 'What do you mean, is it falling off or something? Did you curse it with a vampire's kiss?'

'No, of course not! Oh never mind, you annoying…you little…you annoying boy!' said Sooz.

'Eh?' said a bemused Dirk.

'Oh, never mind, let's go. We've got a meeting, haven't we?' said Sooz, and off she marched, her big Goth boots stomping along.

What have I done now? thought Dirk to

himself as he followed her out.

Moments later, he was walking into Christopher's room. Rufino, Rosapina and Chris were waiting for him. As soon as Dirk crossed the threshold, Christopher stood up angrily and pointed a finger at Dirk.

'You lied to me!' said Chris. 'My mother was never kidnapped!

'And your point is?' said Dirk.

'Well…umm…you're a lying liar!' said Chris,

'Uh-huh. And?' said Dirk.

Chris shook his head. 'Oh, what's the use? You'll never understand,' he said.

'It's beyond his limited understanding. He only thinks of himself and his schemes,' said Sooz waspishly.

'Hey, I was only trying to help!' said Dirk.

'Help yourself get back on your throne, more like!' said Sooz.

Dirk stared at Sooz, for once lost for words. By the Nine Hells, it seemed he'd managed to make all his friends angry with him, thought Dirk. What's the matter with them? Or was it him? No…no, of course not, it couldn't be him, could it?

'We don't have time for this. Come, sit,' said Rosapina, following the exchange with wide eyes. 'We must discuss strategy.'

Sooz and Dirk sat down.

'So, to summarise,' began Rosapina, 'we are at war with the Darklands. Again. They have allied with the Clans of the Undead. They are massing on the Borderlands, with Orcs, Goblins, ghouls, zombies and vampires. We can expect a night assault very soon and we can expect that assault to be augmented with earth technology. Is there anyway we can get any earth weapons ourselves?'

'Not really,' said Dirk. 'Grousammer has had much longer than us to prepare and in any case, he has sealed off the planes, so we cannot get to earth even if we wanted to – only a Storm Crow can.'

'Is there anything you could teach us in the meantime?' said Rosapina.

Dirk blinked. 'Actually, yes. I've learned about gunpowder and ballistics and stuff. Except… well, we probably haven't got enough time.'

'You are wasting what time there is,' said Chris, his face back to the serene peace usually associated with the Holy One. As long as he wasn't angry at Dirk, that was.

'What do you mean?' said Dirk.

'War is evil. Violence is wrong. We must make peace,' said Christopher.

'We've tried that, several times, your Holiness,' said Rosapina. 'Every proposal has been rejected. We even offered to cede them the Borderlands if they'd send the dead home and make peace.'

'Grousammer does not want peace. He knows he can win. He wants war!' said Rufino.

'We just haven't offered him the right terms yet,' said Christopher.

'Short of half of us killing ourselves, the

other half offering up their necks to the Lords of Sunless Keep, and handing over the entire Commonwealth to this Headmaster of Doom, I can't think of any terms he would accept!' said Rufino.

'You just need to get me a face-to-face meeting with Grousammer. I'm sure I can persuade him,' said Chris.

Rufino and Rosapina looked at Chris. Despite their objections, his aura of holy goodness made them want to believe it was possible. Even Sooz looked like she wanted to believe.

To Dirk, though, it sounded absurd. Grousammer had the upper hand, why should he negotiate?

'We've suggested a face-to-face meeting under a flag of truce, but the Dark Lord refused…' said Rosapina.

'Hey, don't call him that! I'm the real Dark Lord, he's just the Headmaster of Doom, or whatever he wants to call himself,' said Dirk.

'Sorry, sorry, as you wish,' said Rosapina.

'Are you really sure you could persuade him, though?' said Sooz to Chris. 'If you sat down with him? Last time it didn't work out like that. There was a huge fight!'

'I know,' said Chris, 'but he attacked my friend, set me off. This time it'll be a flag of truce. I can talk him round. He will see the wisdom of my words and the truth in my heart.'

'All very well, but what's the point if you can't even set up a meeting?' said Dirk.

'Well, I've been thinking about that. Maybe the problem is the person doing the asking. What if you were the intermediary, if you tried to set it up? I mean, you're both…well, dark, right?' said Chris.

'Hah! Don't be ridiculous, Grousammer hates me more than…' Dirk paused. He put a hand up to his chin. 'Wait a minute…' His eyes began to glaze over. He reached into his pocket with his other hand, and felt for the other Anathema

Crystal Hasdruban had left for him. He rolled it round in his hand.

'Hmmm…' he muttered.

Rosapina was about to say something but Rufino put a hand on her arm. 'Hold on. He's plotting,' he whispered. 'Let's see what he comes up with.'

Dirk's face lit up with an evil grin and he chuckled. Not a 'Mwah, hah, hah' but an actual almost human-sounding chuckle.

'I know – let's invite him to tea!' said Dirk.

By Invitation Only

Dirk put the finishing touches to the message and strapped it to Dave's leg. 'There you go, Dave, fly to the Iron Tower and deliver it to that fraudulent old frog, the Headmaster of Doom!'

Dave the Storm Crow squawked loudly and flew like an arrow out of Dirk's room.

Well, then, he thought to himself, the hook is cast! This is what he had sent:

My Dear Grousammer,
You Are Cordially Invited To Afternoon Tea
With The White Wizard. Christopher

A couple of hours later, Dave the Storm Crow flew back through the window to land on Dirk's shoulder with a more tired squawk. Dirk peeled off the message wrapped around his leg, and then gave him some Wormy Wyrms from his jar, and a saucer of milk to which he'd added a little pepper. Dave loved pepper.

Dirk unfurled the reply from Grousammer.

Dirk Lloyd,

Have you any idea how many school rules you have broken? Absent without leave, stealing livestock from the school stables, playing truant, disobeying your headmaster, not stopping when asked to by a prefect, walking on the quadrangle grass, running in the corridor, trespassing in the Borstal Wing ... I could go on! I take a dim view of your

antics, my boy, a dim view, I tell you!
And now, what is this new flim-flammery?
Afternoon tea? It seems far too civilised for
a boy of your troubled background. I must
confess it is intriguing but what would be
the point?

Hercules Grousammer,
The Headmaster of Doom, rightful Dark
Lord and Master of the Darklands.

Dirk grinned his evil grin. Nearly got him. He knew Grousammer, knew his snobby, retro-loving heart. He pulled out the next invitation he had made, just for this occasion.

Vintage Tea and Cakes!
In Our Royal Pavillion, just like the Ritz or
the Savoy back home in the 1950s

He added another note and just to round it off, signed it as Chris.

My Dear Grousammer,
There's nothing like vintage tea and cakes,
1950s style! We'll set up a Royal Pavillion in
the Borderlands and serve the best vintage
high tea ever. It'll be like you really were
at the Ritz or the Savoy back on earth!
And then we can discuss the situation and
whether we can reach common ground.
Yours honestly,
Christopher Purejoie, the White Wizard

Dirk wrapped the paper around Dave's leg. The Storm Crow was staring at him. He cocked his head and squawked as if to say, 'Really? Another one?'

Dirk shrugged. 'I'm afraid so, Dave, but this is the last one, I promise.'

Dave squawked and hopped from foot to foot, looking for all the world like an angry Sooz. He ruffled his feathers but finally flew out of the window once more, still squawking in outrage.

Dirk waited. He went outside and took a walk in the White Tower with Sooz. The garden was quite beautiful – full of pretty flowers and heavenly scents, little arboreal nooks and blossoming crannies. Sooz and Dirk paused in front of a magnificent white rose bush.

'Wrong colour,' said Dirk.

'Yeah,' said Sooz. 'Imagine if they were all black roses.'

'Right – that'd be cool, maybe some of them with the occasional blood red petal too.'

'Hah, nice!' said Sooz and they smiled at each other.

Out of the sky came Dave the Storm Crow, squawking in fatigue, breaking up their nice little moment together. He landed on Dirk's shoulder and slumped there. Dirk reached up and stroked his feathers.

'Well done, my Storm Crow, well done. You can have some worms and we'll get you some of those biscuits from the wizard's lobby,' said Dirk.

Dave crowed in appreciation as Sooz unwrapped the message from his leg.

Greetings, White Wizard,

I have to admit your offer of High Tea sounds rather darkly delightful. I'm not sure that we have much to discuss but I do feel at home with the trappings of the upper classes and their superior manners. A little bit of 'tea at the Ritz' here in the Darklands sounds very pleasant indeed. It's where I belong really, in a high-class establishment, having afternoon tea. Don't you agree? Anyway, my terms – you and me, no more than three retainers each and a full spread of vintage tea and cakes.
See you tomorrow in the Borderlands!

Hercules Grousammer,
The Headmaster of Doom, rightful Dark Lord and Master of the Darklands

'Hah, hah, he's gone for it. I knew the deluded

snob wouldn't be able to resist it!' said Dirk.

'But for what?' said Sooz. 'Isn't this just peace talks?'

'You'll see, Sooz, you'll see!' said Dirk with a mischievous wink.

'Look, Dirk, if this goes wrong it could mean the death of thousands of people – millions, if they get to earth! You do realise that, don't you?' she said.

'Don't worry, Sooz, I've got this covered,' said Dirk.

'Riiight…' said Sooz. 'Just tell me the plan, and I'll be the judge of that.'

'Best not to,' said Dirk. 'The less everyone knows the better, or they might give it away.'

'Give it away? Why would any of us do that?' said Sooz.

'Not deliberately! No, by accident, with the wrong expression or just saying something in the wrong way,' said Dirk.

'We're that stupid, are we? Is that what you're

saying?' said an irritated-sounding Sooz.

'No, no, honestly, it's just that sort of plan. Anyone could give it away, even me, so it's best to keep the knowledge of it down to a minimum,' said Dirk.

Sooz crossed her arms. 'You'd better get this right, Dirk. You really had better.'

Tea for Two

It was a glorious summer's day, and the Royal Pavilion had been set up in a pleasant meadow near a small wood in the Borderlands. Birdsong sounded from the trees and the sun blazed down, soothing all who felt its touch into a drowsy torpor.

Inside the pavilion, a magnificent high tea was laid out on a round table covered in an embroidered damask cloth, with pure silver utensils, cake stands and cruets, and white bone china tea pots and plates beautifully engraved in gold. There were platters of sandwiches, several sorts of cake and a selection of teas.

At the table sat the White Wizard, also called the Holy One, Christopher Purejoie. Behind him stood his retainers, the Paladin Rufino, the Moon Queen Susan Black and Dirk Lloyd, the boy with a chequered past.

At the opposite edge of the table sat Hercules Grousammer, the Headmaster of Doom and the Dark Lord of the Iron Tower. Behind him stood his retainers, the Black Hag, Skabber Stormfart and Oksana, the Dread Mistress of the Underworld – or at least Lucina, the shape-changing Lamia, pretending to be her.

Outside, birds sang in the trees, and bees buzzed in the sunlight. Flies gathered around Skabber.

Dirk stood with arms folded. 'Before we start, do you mind?' he said, gesturing irritably at his mother.

'What?' said Grousammer, turning to look up

at her. 'Oh, yes, of course,' he said with a sly grin, and he waved his hand. 'Oksana' reverted to her normal form as a Lamia, snake-bodied and woman-headed. She smiled at Dirk, chuckling a sibilant chuckle. Grousammer sniggered and the Black Hag cackled.

'Yes, yes, you fooled me, very funny. Now, can we get on with it, please?' said Dirk.

'Of course,' said Grousammer, 'let's have tea!'

Rufino leant forward, pointing to the various pots and plates. 'This is the best tea set in the Commonwealth,' said Rufino. 'It dates back seven hundred years to the rule of Pollus the Polite, a particularly cultured wizard who loved his high teas.'

'I remember him,' said Dirk, 'he... ah... actually...' His voice tailed off.

The Black Hag leant forward and whispered something into the headmaster's ear.

'Aha!' said Grousammer. 'The Lady Grieve tells me that you, Dirk Lloyd, when you were the Dark Lord, put something into his tea, and knocked him out!'

'Did I? Really? Well that was so long ago – I was a different person then, really I was!' said Dirk.

The headmaster narrowed his eyes suspiciously. 'You wouldn't be so stupid as to try that again now, would you?'

'No, no, of course not,' said Dirk, shaking his head.

Rufino tried to change the subject. 'And this plate, my Lord,' said Rufino, picking up a beautifully glazed plate engraved with gold, 'once belonged to Eructator the Engineer, the wizard who built the White Tower, hundreds of years ago.'

'Shall I smash plate, sir?' said Skabber Stormfart with a gormless Orcish chuckle.

Grousammer turned to him, annoyed. 'No you won't smash it, you mindless cretin! It's far too valuable.'

Skabber flinched visibly at the ticking off and rubbed his buttocks.

Rufino glanced over with a querulous look. 'Must you do that?' he muttered.

'My bum's sore,' mumbled Skabber. 'Six of the best!' And he nodded at the Headmaster of Doom.

'What did you do?' Rufino hissed back.

'He failed in his duty, is what he did! Failed to stop that wretched boy riding away,' said the Dark Headmaster, gesturing at Dirk with his cane. 'On a stolen horse, I might add!'

'I sent the horse back,' said Dirk, defiantly. 'And anyway, it's not your horse, it's mine!'

Grousammer surged to his feet. 'When will it sink in, you odious little anarchist? You are not the Dark Lord here any more, I am, and you are nothing but an insignificant boy of maleficent provenance!'

'Insignificant! I am the rightful ruler of all that you have taken. I built it myself, with these hands,' shouted Dirk.

Chris made a face at that, as if to say, 'Well, technically…' but Grousammer pre-empted him.

'Enough of this! What was I thinking? I'm wasting my time here. Come, let us go – soon we will unleash the zomboy apocalypse upon them and all this will seem like an absurd dream!'

'Zombie!' said Dirk. 'Zombie apocalypse.'

As Grousammer was turning to go, Chris rose to his feet. 'Wait. Wait, Headmaster, you must listen to what I have to say, the fate of all our peoples hangs in the balance!'

'Hah, there is no balance, you are doomed to fail, and we to triumph, your people will die as slaves and earth will feed the numberless hordes of the dead that the Clans will become! And I will rule over all. There is nothing more to be said,' boomed the Headmaster of Doom.

Dirk put a hand to his mouth. Had he blown it by losing his temper like that? His plan was beginning to slip out of his control. What an idiot he was, provoking Grousammer like that.

'Just a second, Headmaster,' said Sooz, stepping forward. 'You haven't even had any tea yet. And look at those cakes and cucumber sandwiches. Surely the apocalypse can wait a little longer?'

Grousammer paused. Dirk held his breath.

'After all,' said Sooz, 'once you've unleashed the zomboy apocalypse there'll never be a high tea again. Not like this. Not ever again. Will there?'

Grousammer blinked. 'That true, that's true.' He rubbed his red, raw chin. 'Fine, fine, you're right,' he said, sitting back down, 'but don't think this will get you out of punishment for your long list of misdemeanours, young lady!'

'Of course not, I've got thousands and thousands of lines to write out, I'm sure. I've been very bad!'

Grousammer looked up at her and scowled.

He must have known Susan Black was nearly as tricky as Dirk Lloyd – and that was saying something! Rufino again tried to move things on, handing him the menu, which Grousammer snatched.

White Tower High Tea Menu

A selection of finger sandwiches

Cucumber and elvish cream cheese
Smoked White Lake salmon and dill
mustard
Interplanar egg mayonnaise with chopped
shallots and watercress

Good folk pastries and cakes

Fruits of the elvish forest and chocolate
gateaux
Strawberry tart a la Skirrit

Buttered crumpets with Blood Bean jam

<u>*Selection of teas*</u>

Earl White Tea
White Tower Breakfast Blend
Wizard Tea
Bitter Borderlands Blend

'Hmmm…' said Grousammer, perusing the menu. 'I'll have the Bitter Borderlands, I think!'

'Of course, Headmaster,' said Rufino, playing the waiter to perfection, leaning over and pouring the tea into the headmaster's cup. 'And for you, your Holiness?' said Rufino, turning to Christopher.

'Whatever you think is best, Rufino. I've no time for tea! We've got far more important things to discuss, such as how to resolve this situation without bloodshed,' said Chris in a calm, peaceful voice. 'What do you think, Headmaster?'

Grousammer leant forward and poured a little milk into his tea. 'Bloodshed? What do I care if my Orcs and Goblins shed their blood!' At that, Skabber frowned in disgust…but the Dark Headmaster continued. 'And as for the rest of my army, they will be drinking your people's blood!'

'But there's no need for any of that,' said Christopher earnestly. 'Don't you see that violence is wrong, that it doesn't solve anything and only creates cycles of further violence, just like what's been going on here with these endless wars between the Commonwealth and the Darklands?'

Grousammer spooned some sugar into his teacup and stirred. 'This time, though, I've got the Clans of the Undead. And all that stuff I brought over from earth. This time violence is going to solve everything because we're going to crush you utterly and I will rule over what remains of your people for ever and ever!' He stared wildly at Chris, jutting out his chin, before raising his cup of tea to his lips, a bony, taloned little finger sticking out to the side elegantly.

Dirk sucked in his breath in anticipation but at the last moment, Grousammer paused.

'Wait a minute,' he said. 'I'm not drinking any of this until after you've had a sip! Not after that story about Pollus the Polite getting poisoned!'

'What?' said Christopher. 'I'm not interested in tea, for goodness sake! We need to find some common ground, to resolve this peacefully. I'm sure we can – we have to, to avoid bloodshed. Don't you see that?'

'Don't you see that half of my army needs blood to be shed just so they can go on living? Well, technically they're not alive anyway, but you take my point, right?' said Grousammer.

'Come now,' said Chris exuding the most

calming, loving, kind, peaceful aura of gentleness. 'Can't we come to some kind of accommodation?'

Around him, Sooz, Rufino, Skabber and the Lamia Lucina were all affected in some way. They smiled peacefully and nodded. Surely there would be peace? They could live together, harmoniously. Love would prevail. Even the Black Hag frowned in puzzlement as if she were feeling something she hadn't felt in many years. Only Dirk and Grousammer remained unaffected.

Grousammer drummed the table with his fingers. 'Look, are you going to drink your tea? I'd really like to try it myself. The same with those sandwiches and cakes, but I'm not touching anything until you do.'

'How can you think of tea and cakes at such a moment?' said Chris.

'Bah, what a sanctimonious fool you have turned out to be, Christopher Purejoie! Had I known what your vocational choices were going to be, I would have expelled you immediately,' said the Headmaster of Doom.

Dirk stepped forward and said to Christopher, 'Why not have some tea, your Holiness? Perhaps if Grousammer has some tea and cake that will put him in a better mood?'

'Hah,' said Grousammer. 'Good advice from the chief delinquent of all delinquents! Sip your tea, take a bite out of one of those cucumber sandwiches, and have a slice of gateau. I'm eager to try those myself!'

Christopher sighed. 'And if I do, will you discuss peace terms?'

'Oh, of course, of course! We can discuss them, sure!' said Grousammer exchanging a look with Lucina the Lamia – a 'what an idiot he is' look, that everyone else could see except Christopher.

'Well, all right, then,' said Chris, and he took a sip of his tea. And then a little more. Then he took a bite of a sandwich.

'No, not that one! I hate fish. That one, the cucumber and elvish cream cheese. I want to try that,' said Grousammer.

'Oh, I see, terribly sorry,' said Chris, grabbing a cucumber sandwich and taking a bite out of it. 'Mmm, that's actually pretty good,' said Chris. 'Cheesy!' He wolfed the rest of it down.

'Good, good. Now the cake. Go on, the chocolatey one,' said the Headmaster of Doom.

Chris raised his eyes. 'All right, all right.' And he took a slice of cake and ate a mouthful, before putting it back down.

Grousammer stared at him. Nothing happened. Chris raised his eyebrows.

'Fine!' said Grousammer and he grabbed a cucumber sandwich and took a bite himself.

'Hah, finally, something we can agree on,' said the Headmaster. 'They are indeed excellent!'

Then he took a slice of gateau and, using a small silver fork, delicately ate a mouthful or two. 'Mmm…' he mumbled as he slurped another sip of tea, his fine manners beginning to break down in the face of such yumminess.

Dirk couldn't help himself – a slow grin began to take shape on his face. Grousammer narrowed his eyes suspiciously.

'What are you grinning about, boy?' he said.

And then Christopher began to choke…

Storm in a Teacup

Christopher put a hand up to his throat and let out a gargled cry of distress.

Grousammer surged to his feet once more. 'Aiiieee! Poison!' was all he could get out. Behind him, Skabber reached for his sharpened steel ruler, the Black Hag crouched, hands out, iron talons at the ready, and Lucina the Lamia reared back, ready to change at any moment.

Sooz looked over at Dirk, who was smiling. But Rufino, who clearly had no idea what was going on, stepped forward and slapped Chris on the back.

'No, no, of course not, we wouldn't poison the Holy One just to poison you, now would we? I'm sure it's just some tea gone down the wrong way,' he said, giving Chris another slap on the back.

Grousammer hesitated. 'I'd put poison in everyone's tea, just to get one of you, of course, but… No, you lot wouldn't do that, would you?' he said.

But Christopher still wasn't all right. Suddenly he stood up, put his hands on the table. 'Something…wrong…inside…' he said through gritted teeth.

And then Grousammer started to choke. 'Wait…you did! You poisoned us both. How could you…?' shrieked Grousammer, pointing a bony hand at Dirk.

Dirk put his head back and let loose a mighty 'Mwah, hah, hah!' that echoed around the tent.

Grousammer staggered. 'Kill them! Kill them all,' he said to his retainers. The Black Hag hissed and stepped forward, claws at the ready. Lucina began changing into a big, powerful ogre and Rufino readied himself for battle. They were outnumbered. Things were looking bad when Skabber stepped up next to Rufino.

'If that Dark Lord's on the way out, well, I figures I'll fight for the old one, even if he is a human kid,' he said.

Rufino grinned and slapped the big Orc on the back, whilst Lucina and the Black Hag bared their teeth and growled. Now they were the outnumbered ones!

'Gah…' croaked Grousammer. 'It'll be 666 of the best for you next time, Skabber!'

The Black Hag, Lucina, Rufino and Skabber were squaring off against each other when Dirk said, 'Enough, you idiots, it's already over! I ground an Anathema Crystal up, put it in the tea and cake. I bet you didn't prepare for that, eh, Headmaster? Bet you've got no protection against a crystal you've ingested, rather than just shattered in the usual way, eh?' said a grinning Dirk.

The Holy One and the Headmaster of Doom looked at each other, their eyes widening in shocked surprise.

'NOOOOOooooooooooo!' they both said at the same time.

And then Christopher vomited – all over the tea table. And his vomit was white, a pure ultraviolet white that sprayed all over the tea and cakes.

'Essence of Good!' said Sooz, as Lucina and the Black Hag reared backward in disgust. Christopher began to shrink, rapidly turning back into a blonde-haired, blue-eyed thirteen-year-old boy from Sussex.

Grousammer's eyes rolled up into his head. His head fell back and then rocked forward suddenly, his mortarboard flying through the air and hitting Dirk on the head. A stream of black liquid was vomited out of the headmaster's mouth, black and glistening. It too splashed on to the tea table.

'Essence of Evil!' said Sooz.

Dirk, momentarily stunned, a gash over one eye where the corner of the mortarboard had caught him, shook his head to clear his vision, and saw the Headmaster of Doom reverting rapidly to his original form too – a tall, gangly fellow with dark red hair, a square face and a long, craggy nose. His tattered clothes had turned back into a raggedy old green suit – the same one he used to wear when he was headmaster of Whiteshields School back on earth – his deadly cane now a simple old walking stick.

He sat on the floor, a bemused expression on his face. And then his expression hardened and he scowled angrily. 'Curse you, Lloyd, you little fiend, curse you! I loved being the Headmaster of Doom. It was my destiny, my fate to rule!' He scrabbled to his feet, and lurched over to the table, hands ready to scoop up the Essence of Evil and slurp it back down.

Except that it wasn't there any more. The Essence of Good and the Essence of Evil had joined together on the table to form a large, gloopy pile of grey sludge. Grousammer stared down at it.

'Wha—' was all he could get out.

'Hah, Essence of…hmm…what, exactly?' said Sooz.

'Neutrality?' said Rufino.

'Disinterested amorality?' said Dirk.

'Essence of Sitting on the Fence, perhaps,' added Sooz.

Everyone stood and stared at the pile of grey goo for a moment, forgetting all their enmities and disagreements. It seemed to exude a feeling of…world-weary laziness – a feeling of not being bothered or not doing anything because it wasn't really worth the trouble.

'Well…what now?' said Lucina the Lamia,

seeming to snap out of her lethargy.

'Now everyone goes home. You can't go on without the Headmaster of Doom. The Clans of the Undead will return to Sunless Keep in the Deadlands. The Orcs and Goblins will look to their original leader – me! I'll sit on the throne once more,' said Dirk.

'Good,' said Skabber. 'Me ready to serve, my Lord!'

Lucina and the Black Hag exchanged a look.

'So be it,' croaked the Black Hag in a voice like sand.

'What about me?' whimpered Grousammer.

'You're going back with us to earth, where you can get a proper job!' said Sooz.

'A job? Noooo, anything but that!' said Grousammer

'Whatever,' said Sooz. 'I've had enough. Let's get out of here… Which way, though – the White Tower or the Iron Tower?'

Dirk put a hand to his chin. 'Actually, I don't

really know!' he said. He felt something on his finger. The Great Ring! It had come back to life, its runes writhing with a fiery glow. Dirk's heart filled with exultation. He was the rightful Dark Lord once more.

'I think perhaps the Iron Tower, after all,' said Dirk.

Epilogue

Dirk was standing outside the school gates waiting for Chris and Sooz, who were walking down the lane towards him. It was the first day back at school, and also the first time they'd had a chance to talk properly since the events in the Royal Pavilion back in the Darklands.

Dirk walked up to greet his friends. 'Good to have you back, your Holiness,' said Dirk, putting an arm around Chris and grinning madly.

But Chris shrugged him off. 'Hey, I'm not the

Holy One any more – and I haven't forgiven you! You tricked me, turned me into the White Wizard, after I told you not to!'

'Hey, sorryyyy for saving the world – again!' said Dirk, throwing his hands in the air.

'And what about me?' said Sooz. 'You locked me in the top of the White Tower, and because of that I ended up locked in the bottom of the Iron Tower! You're the worst – a lying liar and a tricksy trickster!'

'Well, it all turned out right in the end, didn't it?'

'Turned out right? Hah, easy for you to say. You weren't turned into some kind of holy wotsit and surrounded by an army of ravenous vampires!' said Chris.

'Or tied up in chains and thrown into a dungeon!' said Sooz.

'Oh, come on, I still saved you both!' said Dirk.

'Please, don't pretend like we owe you now,'

said Chris, raising his eyes.

A figure slowly walked towards them. It was Grousammer – now the school janitor after Hasdruban had shown mercy and given him a job (as much to keep an eye on him as anything else).

The three of them stopped and stared at him as he approached but he ignored them.

'I could have been king of the world...' muttered Grousammer to himself as he shambled by.

Dirk smiled wryly. Sooz shook her head and got back to the discussion they were having. 'So, wait – you get someone imprisoned and then free them but expect them to remember only the bit where you let them out?' said Sooz.

'Well...you know, it was all part of my master plan. No one died or anything, right?' said Dirk.

'Your master plan? The one that kept going wrong!' said Chris.

'It went right in the end, though!' said Dirk.

They fell silent, glaring at each other, arguments exhausted.

'Leader of the Unfree World. Could have been me,' they could just hear Grousammer mumble, holding up his old walking stick as he shuffled through the school gates.

Sooz, Chris and Dirk exchanged looks. They couldn't help themselves. They started to laugh.

From a second-storey window a white-bearded head leaned out – the headmaster, old Hasdruban.

'Come on, children, it's time to sign in!' he said in his kindly voice.

'Yes, Headmaster!' said the Dark Lord, the Moon Queen and the Holy One together. They turned and headed through the school gates, grinning at each other happily.

THE END

If you liked

DARK LORD

you will love ...

978-1-40833-026-5

978-1-40833-030-2

1 BIRTHDAY BOY

'**AAARGHHHH!**' bellowed Harry at the top of his lungs. A figure with a heart-shaped face, great big black eyes and a head like a fungus-covered grey turnip had just loomed over him. Harry, terrified at the sight, tried to get up, but he couldn't move. Two more turnip heads followed. Hideous nightmare turnip heads that were clearly not human! Harry began to panic as he struggled harder to get up – why couldn't he move? He looked down – he was lying on a table in the middle of an antiseptic white room. He looked back up at the strange creatures. They were scary for sure, but they also reminded him of something…what was it? Greys! That was it. Greys, those aliens he'd seen in films, the ones that were always abducting people and carrying them off! Ridiculous, of course, I mean, why would aliens come all this way just to carry off…wait a minute!

Harry blinked, staring at the Greys. Come all this way just to carry *him* off... Why would they... Harry gulped. What could they possibly want with a fourteen-year-old boy from Croydon?

'What do you want? Who are you? No, wait, what are you???' he demanded in panicky tones.

At this, the Greys started muttering to each other in voices like croaky mosquito whines. It reminded him of his mate Harvey, who whined and moaned whenever Harry beat him in a game.

One of the Greys tapped a little headset device attached to the side of its head.

'Please lie still, human thing,' it said.

'Don't tell me what to do, you…thing! You turnip thing!' blustered Harry. He was actually rather terrified, but he wasn't going to let them know that.

Another Grey came over to the table. From the way the others immediately hunched over, this one seemed to be in charge. It said something to the one who had spoken to Harry, then pointed with a long snaky finger at a screen on the wall.

Harry stretched his neck so he could see the screen. It was weird, because he was looking past his feet at the screen, but the image on the screen showed the exact same view of his feet, and then him looking at another screen in that. Hundreds of pairs of feet, stretching off to infinity.

Read Wrong Side of the Galaxy *to find out what happens next.*